DIRTY
PLEASURES

Book Two of the The Dirty Billionaire Trilogy

Meghan March

ABOUT THIS BOOK

I did it. I married a billionaire.

My reasons are my own, but the last thing I expected was to feel owned. I may have taken vows, but I'm still determined to be me.

Now his rules are taking over my world, but I'm not the kind of girl to just obey.

There's only one problem: I might actually be falling for him.

I have no idea how this marriage is going to go, but holding on to a piece of myself while succumbing to his dirty pleasures is shaping up to be the ride of a lifetime.

Dirty Pleasures is the second book in The Dirty Billionaire Trilogy and should be read following *Dirty Billionaire*. The story concludes in *Dirty Together*.

ACKNOWLEDGMENTS

It takes a fabulous team to coax a spark of an idea along the twisty and crazy path to becoming a finished novel, and I'm lucky to have an amazing one.

Special thanks go out to:

Angela Smith of Grey Ghost Author Services, LLC, my amazing PA and best friend. It's been a wild and crazy ride, but this is only the beginning. I'm so proud of you and blessed to have you in my life.

Angela Marshall Smith and Pam Berehulke, editors extraordinaire, for once again helping me deliver the best story I'm capable of writing.

Chasity Jenkins-Patrick, kick-ass publicist, for talking me off more than one ledge and always pushing me in the right direction.

Natasha Gentile, for being a fabulous beta reader. Love your messages, lady!

Sara Eirew for shooting a fab cover pic, and By Hang Le for the absolutely gorgeous cover design.

The Meghan March Runaway Readers Facebook group, for being the most fabulous collection of ladies I've had the pleasure of (virtually) meeting. Hope to hug you all at events soon!

All the book bloggers who take the time to read and review this and any of my other books. Your time and dedication are truly appreciated.

My readers—I'm infinitely grateful that you've picked up this book. Without you, I wouldn't be living my dream.

CHAPTER ONE

Holly

BILLIONAIRE'S BRIDE FLYING COACH?

Holly Wix, newly married to billionaire Creighton Karas, was spotted on a commercial flight from NYC to Nashville, and our sources say she was flying coach. Is there trouble in paradise already? With a fleet of three Gulfstreams, you'd think the billionaire could have arranged a classier ride for his bride. We'll be reporting back when we have more on the latest match to rock Music City.

The cab ride to the airport took the rest of my cash, and I'm lucky that I'm getting paid next week, because the last-minute flight maxed out my own credit card. I left my new Amex Black Card on the kitchen counter of my new husband's Fifth Avenue penthouse.

Big sunglasses hide the circles under my eyes, and hopefully my identity. I thought I saw a guy on his phone staring at me a little too long, but I'm not worrying about it. I shouldn't be that recognizable. This town is full of one-hit wonders, and I haven't even had a chart-topping single yet. Plus, without all my stage makeup on and my hair in a messy braid, I just look like your average Midwestern girl.

I stretch, trying to work out the knots in my back after sitting through the flight with my arms practically tucked around my body. My middle seat in coach put me right between two very large men who smelled strongly of garlic. I thought about writing, but I didn't want to move, let alone get my notebook out and have them stare at what I was doing. So I kept myself immobile, which explains the knots in my back.

Anyway, my thoughts were probably too jumbled to do anything more than massacre the song ideas I jotted down today while I waited for Creighton. I know I have a good one percolating, but it's still just out of reach. I can't find the right words quite yet, which might be to blame on my mental state.

But the upside is I'm back in Nashville, and Tana's Range Rover is idling at the curb when I step out of the sliding glass doors of the airport.

The window slides down as she waves me over. "Get your ass in here before I get towed!"

I smile, relieved to feel a little of my shitty mood slipping away. Opening the door, I slide inside.

"Your luggage get lost?" She surveys the one small bag

I shove down by my feet.

"Nope. This is it."

Her eyebrows shoot up. "Oh, please God, tell me that he made you go naked and that's why you have no clothes other than the ones you probably wore when you flew to New York on New Year's Eve."

Tana was aware of every intimate detail of my trip, and disagreed with my choice to bring nothing but myself.

I smile at her expression. "No naked rule. I just . . . felt like traveling light."

Her eyebrows fall back into their normal position and her smile slips into a frown. "Please don't tell me this has something to do with your mom and her hooking up with every man in town and letting them pay her way."

And *that's* the joy of having a friend who has plied you with enough wine to spill your whole life story. But in this instance, she's not exactly right. The reasons I left New York are a lot bigger than that.

"Tana—"

"Damn it, Holly. I knew this was going to happen. I *knew* it."

I really don't want to have this conversation now, because Tana will want to dissect not only what happened with Creighton, but why I'm acting the way I am. I'm too worried about missing the bus to play along while she psychoanalyzes my actions in light of what she knows about my past. I love her, but I just can't right now. So I tell her the truth.

"Can we hold off on this conversation until I'm not on the edge of being late for a tour bus leaving? I really, really just want to get to my apartment and grab my stuff so I can get on the bus and forget about everything but the music."

"You're not missing the friggin' bus. I'll get you home as quick as a cab would." She gives me a side-eye. "But you're gonna talk while I drive."

I sigh and stare straight ahead as she pulls away from the curb and waves to the security guy eyeing her car suspiciously. Her head jerks toward me before she focuses once again on navigating through airport traffic.

"Talk, woman."

"What do you want me to say?"

"That your husband knows exactly where you are, and you're not a runaway bride."

"Har-har. I'm hardly a runaway bride. That requires running away before the vows, I think."

She cuts through my bullshit answer. "Does your husband know where you are?"

I fix my stare on the red light as we slow. "I left a note."

"Which said?"

I should have known Tana wouldn't drop it. She's a damn bulldog about getting the details. If she weren't my closest and possibly only friend, I'd tell her to back off. But instead, I tell her the truth.

"It said good-bye." My reply is a mumble, because I know I'm about to get a verbal bitch-slapping.

Her screech, which is oddly melodic, fills the cabin of the Range Rover. "Why would you do that? Did he hit you?"

I swing my head to face her. "No! Of course not!" I can't believe she'd even ask that.

She glances back at me before her eyes go back to the road, and we accelerate. "So then, what happened? He's a billionaire, so maybe he was into that kinky Christian Grey stuff? Did he have a Red Room of Pain? Oh my God, he did, didn't he? Did he spank you? Bring out his riding crop? Shit. That's hot."

I cover my face with my palm. I don't even know where to start, but I have to say something or she'll keep going. Her imagination is just getting fired up. And God knows I don't want her to actually hit on the truth.

But how do I answer that? He did spank me, and I loved it. And then the . . . other stuff. Kinky billionaire, indeed.

"He didn't get out a riding crop, and there was no Red Room of Pain."

Thankfully, the answer stops her tide of kinky questions.

Shaking her head, she replies, "Well, that's just damn disappointing. So, are you just crazy? Who walks out on a billionaire with a note that just says good-bye? Oh, and doesn't bring anything with her? That's evidence of crazy right there, if I've ever seen any."

I decide that the truth is all I can offer in my defense. "Look, you know I need to be on that bus or I'm screwed. I couldn't wait any longer, so I did what I had to do." I turn and look at her. "I did exactly what you would've done in my shoes—what was best for my career."

"I would've hitched a ride on a private jet, that's what I would've done. Girl, you've gotta learn to use what you've been given to your best advantage."

Her words crack something open inside me and the truth spills out.

"Well, I couldn't exactly hop a ride on the private jet because he forgot about me." At her look of shock, I continue. "Yeah, that's right. My husband forgot about me. Told me when he'd be there, and he wasn't. And not only was he not there, he didn't answer my calls or texts, so finally I got through to his number-two guy and basically got the blow-off speech. So that's what happened. End of story."

"Oh shit, honey. I'm sorry. That ain't cool at all." Sympathy coats her every word.

"Well, it's not like I'm the most important piece on the chessboard he calls an empire."

Tana looks at me sideways as we merge onto the highway. "But, honey, you're his queen. I don't know jack shit about chess, but is there a more important piece on the board to the king?"

A sick feeling settles in my stomach. "I guess to Creighton, he's the most important piece on the board, and everything else can be sacrificed for the good of the king."

Tana's face falls. "I'm sorry, hon. That sucks big hairy balls. So I guess that means you're not going to call him and let him know you made it, despite not having a fancy jet to fly on, huh?"

I consider it again. I mean, if I were a *real* wife, I'd probably tell him I made it. But honestly, what are the odds that Creighton has even noticed I'm gone yet? He couldn't step away for thirty seconds before.

And then there's the mulishly stubborn part of me holding on to some thin thread of hope that maybe Creighton will call *me*. And then what? Apologize for blowing me off? Tell me he misses me, and he's on his way because he can't stand to be away from me?

Each possibility seems more unlikely than the last.

Tana doesn't ask any other questions as we navigate the traffic and finally pull up in front of my apartment. It's a far cry from the giant mansion on a sprawling estate behind fancy gates like Tana lives in. But that's life as a new kid on the block trying to make it big.

My contract with Homegrown might have sounded impressive when I won the show *Country Dreams*, but "a million-dollar recording contract" doesn't go very far when you consider how much it costs to produce an album. For the hours I put into practicing, writing, doing press, radio spots, and everything else, I barely make minimum wage. On top of that, my cut from concert ticket and album sales is laughable.

Even though it was a rude awakening to find out exactly what I signed with such stars in my eyes, it doesn't bother me as much as you might think. Most of the people I know who didn't get into the business on one of those make-me-a-star TV shows lived in crappier accommodations for a time before they hit it big.

Some even lived in their cars—provided they didn't get repo'd. Jason Aldean's song "Crazy Town" was based in truth. You just never know when or if you're going to "make it." You really could be losing everything one minute and then be getting a fat paycheck the next. It's the game we're all playing and hoping to win. There are no guarantees for any of us.

"Thank you for the ride, babe. You know I appreciate it."

"Of course. You sure you don't want me to stick around?"

I shake my head. "I just need to grab a few things and find out where the bus is parked." Glancing at the time on the dash, I realize I've got less than an hour. "I better get going."

"All right, hon. You break a leg on that stage, hear me? And when that man comes crawling back to you—because if he knows the kind of woman he's got, he'll be doing exactly that—give him a chance."

I swing my head to stare at her. "Give him a chance? I thought you were going to tell me to rip him a new asshole. Why—?"

Tana's blue eyes are sympathetic. "You've got a lot of mistrust built up because of your ma, and you have to realize you're not her. Your life is what you make of it, and I'm still holding out some hope that this guy is worthy of you. Give him a chance to grovel. A man's character has a tendency to get really fucking clear when he's groveling because the best thing that ever happened to him is on the line."

I try to summon a smile, but I can't quite do it. "I guess we'll see if he comes groveling at all." I lean over the center console to hug her. "See you soon."

"Knock 'em dead, hon," Tana says as I slip out of the car.

CHAPTER TWO

Holly

Hurrying, I adjust my purse over my shoulder and hustle up to my apartment. The first thing I see when I open my door is my old battered guitar case tucked under my coffee table.

My first ever. I fried thousands of onion rings and tater tots in order to buy this guitar from Super Pawn. It took me almost a year to save up, and then when I finally had the cash in hand and went to the pawnshop, the owner offered me a disgusting back-office discount.

Furious, I threw the bills on the counter, not bothering to haggle, and told him to give me the damn guitar before I reported him to the cops for soliciting sex with a minor. It was so much less than what I wanted to do—namely, grab the baseball bat from behind the counter and swing it at his head. I left minutes later with my very first guitar and never looked back.

A million years ago, it seems. Just look how much has changed.

I'm halfway down the tiny hallway to my bedroom when my phone buzzes in my purse. *Creighton* is my first thought. My hand shakes as I dig inside to pull it out.

My heart—my stupid heart—falls when I see the text is from my manager.

Chance: Where the hell are you? You better be on your way. BT is almost ready to head out.

Shit. I run into my bedroom and grab a suitcase from my closet, and stuff handfuls of underwear and bras in it. A few pairs of yoga pants and some T-shirts and jeans, and I'm pretty much packed.

I reply to Chance.

Holly: Just finished packing. On my way. Where's the bus?

Chance's answer makes me cringe.

Chance: At BT's. I left your name at the gate.

Double shit. BT is Boone Thrasher—the headliner of the tour I'm currently on. His place isn't in one of those fancy neighborhoods behind a regular gate like Tana's. No, he lives out in the boondocks where he can shoot skeet off his back porch, ride his dirt bikes on his own track, and his dogs can run wild and bark at everything in sight.

If I'm going to get to his place on time, I'll need every minute I've got. I've been there once before, when he invited me out to meet him before agreeing to have me on his tour. He wanted to make sure I wasn't going to be—in his words—*some whiny-ass bitch who would make him miserable*. We hit it off when I kicked his ass at bowling in his basement lane. You can take the girl out of the bowling alley . . .

Time to get my ass in gear and hustle, but my phone buzzes again.

Chance: Good news. He wants to rehearse that duet you talked about before Christmas. Get your ass here and make it happen.

I toss my phone on the bed and do a little fist pump before tearing off my jeans and blouse to throw on something clean and get the hell out of here. This duet would mean getting to go back out onstage during his set where I can feel the energy coming from his fans when they're all whipped up and excited for him.

As the first act, I generally play to a less-than-full stadium, when people are a little more concerned about making sure they have full beers than they are about paying attention to my music. Well, except for the fans who actually come to see *me*.

But this is where everyone starts, I remind myself, and I'm crazy lucky that I'm on tour with Boone Thrasher to begin with. And the duet? That's *huge*.

I spend thirty seconds freshening up my makeup and shoving my toiletries in my makeup bag before slipping into the battered brown-and-black cowboy boots I bought for my eighteenth birthday. Which was the fourth birthday in a row that my mama didn't even bother to send a card.

Pushing that thought away, because it was just one more piece of baggage that Tana was talking about when she dropped me off, I grab my jacket and head for the door.

Despite his badass reputation, Boone's a good guy. A *really* good guy. His tiny, gorgeous, chart-topping girlfriend is a lucky lady. But from what I've seen of her, I'm not so sure she's aware of that fact. She's actually kind of a bitch. And by kind of, I mean, she's a total Grade-A, possessive, catty bitch.

Not that I'd ever tell Boone that. These lips don't do the gossip thing. One negative word to the wrong person, and I'd be screwed. So I just keep my opinions to myself. The world of country music isn't so different from high school.

I lock my apartment door behind me and hoof it down the stairs and out to the covered parking where my 1998 Pontiac Firebird waits for me. And yes, I'm completely aware that what was cool in 1998 is not quite so cool now. Which means that I got a killer deal on it when my 1988 Fiero kicked the bucket just before I got my golden audition ticket for *Country Dreams*.

I suppose I could buy a little bit newer car with the semi-regular paycheck I get now, but the Firebird still gets me from A to B, and I prefer to save my money for a rainy day. If there's one thing that I've learned about this town, it's that everything can change in a moment.

Thirty-five minutes later, I pull up at the gates of Boone's place, and a man built like a brick shithouse comes out of the guard shack and bends down to my window. I open the door—because the window doesn't work anymore—and he smiles.

"I got the same problem with my Grand Prix. Fucking Pontiacs," he says.

"You got that right. I'm Holly—"

"Yep. Know who you are, sweet thing. They're waiting on you. Buses are here and ready to go too." He backs away from my car and activates the gate opener.

I swing my door shut and drive through. Sure enough, two tour buses are parked in front of the house set off from the road by almost a mile-long driveway. I pull into a small parking lot-size area beside the garage and shut off my car.

I need to get in there and find Chance and make sure he reports in that I wasn't late before someone at the label starts checking, looking to boot me off. As soon as the thought hits my brain, the man in question knocks on the window of my car and opens the door.

"You need to replace this piece of shit, girl. And why the hell didn't you answer your phone?"

I frown at Chance. "What are you talking about? I answered your texts."

He pulls me out of my car by the hand. "Well, you didn't answer when I called you five times to ask you to pick me up some Johnny Walker on the way. The bus is out, and Boone wants some for the road."

"Crap. I must've had my radio on too loud. It's on vibrate." I reach back into my car to grab my purse and start rooting through it to find my phone.

"Your suitcase in the trunk?" Chance asks.

I nod, not looking up from my task, and he reaches around me to pop the trunk. By the time he has my suitcase in hand, I'm starting to panic.

"Where the hell is my phone?" I mumble. "I had it."

"Come on, girl. Let's move it. We won't get to San Antonio with you standing here digging through your purse."

I jerk my head up and stare at him. "San Antonio? I thought Dallas was next."

Chance shakes his head. "Nope. That's why we're leaving early. Boone signed up to do a last-minute charity gig, and you're along for the ride. Dallas is after that, so it's not that far off."

Dropping my purse on the ground, I bend over and look between the seats and the console to see if my phone slid down. Chance, clearly impatient with me, calls it. I wait, but there's no telltale buzz or vibration.

"Shit. I must've left it in my apartment."

"No time to go back for it, so you'll have to have someone get it for you and overnight it to you. I'll get the hotel address."

I huff out a long sigh. *Shit.* I don't even know if I have Tana's number to ask her to go back to my place and grab it . . . but then again, I bet Chance or Boone does. Between the two of them, they seem to have everyone's number in this town.

"You ready to rehearse?"

"What?" I ask, my mind still on how to retrieve my phone.

"The duet. 'That Girl.' Boone wants to play some acoustic stuff on the bus, so you're riding with him. I made sure you've got a guitar on there already. Now come on, let's go."

Chance leads me by the arm up to the house to say hi to the guys before we all climb up the stairs. All my worries slip away once I let myself fall into the easy bullshitting and name-calling with the guys. And once I'm on the bus with Boone, I let myself go in the music.

CHAPTER
THREE

Holly

It's a couple of hours and who knows how much whiskey later when we stop so the guys can grab a smoke. I stumble onto my own bus—one that I'll be sharing with my band and maybe the other opening act, if they don't have their own bus. No one has seen fit to share that detail with me yet. But because it's out of my control, I don't waste any more time thinking about it.

Some drunk hope makes me think that maybe I missed my phone in my search of the purse, so I dump the entire contents out on the kitchenette table.

A handful of tampons. A dozen or so lip glosses and lipsticks. A lighter—not sure where that came from, since I don't smoke. My wallet. My car keys. My songwriting notebook. My smaller backup songwriting notebook.

Six pens, in all different colors. Two pencils. Gum. Gum wrappers. Loose change. Lint.

Still no phone.

Before I left Boone's bus, I asked Chance for Tana's number, just in case. He wrote it on my palm in Sharpie with big block letters saying Call Me above it.

I make my way up to the bus driver's seat.

"Hey, Chaz?"

"Ma'am?"

"Told you to call me Holly a dozen times, Chaz." Maybe more than a dozen, if I'm being honest.

"Yes, Ms. Holly."

"Can I borrow your phone?"

"Sure thing." He grabs it from the pocket in the side of his seat and hands it over, all without ever taking his eyes off the road.

"Thanks."

I stumble back to the couch and position my thumb over the number pad. I glance down at my palm, and I know the person I should be calling instead of Tana is Creighton.

But you didn't merit a phone call from him, the hurt inside me protests. It's true, but still.

I drop my head to the back of the couch when it hits me that even if I wanted to call Creighton, I don't know any of his numbers by heart, and it's not like I can just call Information or something. I could google Karas International, but what is the likelihood they'll ever put me through to his personal line? Even when I had that number, his secretary didn't believe that I was me at first.

My best bet is getting my phone back.

I punch in Tana's number, and she answers after I call her three times in a row.

"Hello?" Her voice is suspicious as shit, and I realize she doesn't recognize the number. Plus it's almost midnight.

"It's me. Holly. Sorry for calling so late."

"Oh, hey, hon. No worries. You know I'm up at all hours anyway. What's up? The man come track you down already?"

I squeeze my eyes shut. Hell, even if Creighton wanted to track me down right now, I think even he'd be SOL. I'm on a bus on a highway headed for a tour stop not on my tour list.

But then again, I guess I don't know what kind of resources he has at his disposal, or if he'd use them to come after me. The hope rising in my chest, the hope that started blossoming that night we ate *Sixteen Candles* style on the dining room table, wants desperately for him to come chasing after me with an apology.

"Holly?"

"Sorry, I'm a little whiskey-mellowed right now, and you can blame that on Boone."

"Ooh, that boy is so damn hot. If you weren't married to a billionaire, I'd say you need to snake him from his bitchy girlfriend, even though I strongly disagree with poaching on every level. But that's neither here nor there. So, you call your man yet?"

"No, because I left my phone in my apartment, I think, and all his numbers are on it. Can I ask you a huge favor?"

"Oh shit, and you know you can ask me anything, doll."

"Would you go back to my place in the morning and call it and see if you can find it? And if you do, can you send it to me in Dallas? I can text you the address."

"Sure thing. Although, if I didn't love you quite so much, I'd have to point out that I have a personal assistant who does this kind of crap for me. You owe me, girl. I want an invite to a really fancy party when you and the big billionaire reconcile. Or maybe a week in Paris. I heard he has a place there."

Paris? I didn't know that. "I'm sorry to ask. You know I wouldn't if I had someone else I could trust."

"I'm just giving you a hard time, girl. I'll take care of it in the morning."

"Thank you, Tana."

"This does entitle me to say one thing, though."

I brace myself. "Go on."

"I bet you're wishing now that you wrote more on that note than just 'good-bye.'"

"That's dangerously close to saying 'I told you so.'"

"Sorry, babe. But it's true."

"Maybe he hasn't even realized I'm gone yet," I say, wondering if it might actually be true.

"I imagine that man will find you before you find him," she replies. "He doesn't strike me as the type to have a wife go missing and let it stand for long."

"I guess we'll see."

I hope she's right, and equal measures of dread and hope fill me again. I made a mess of this, but Creighton

19

isn't blameless either.

"I should go," I tell her. "I need to sleep off the whiskey so I can think with a clear head in the morning."

"All right, babe. You do that. Talk soon. Love you."

"Love you too, Tana. Thank you."

We hang up, and I return Chaz's phone to him.

"Thanks, Chaz. I'm going to call it a night."

"Sure thing, ma'am. Sleep well."

I'm too tired to correct him as I make my way to the bedroom in the back of the bus—one I'm surprised none of the guys in the band have claimed. But the curtains of the bunks are all pulled tight, and I'm not about to offer to swap.

I strip off my jeans and slide between the sheets of the queen-sized bed. Without my pajamas, I'm sleeping in just a T-shirt and undies. But considering that the guys have seen me in this and maybe less, I'm not concerned. They're all married or in long-term relationships. Even more than that, they're road warriors with more tours under their belts than I have fingers.

The sound of the tires on the highway lulls me to sleep, and my last thought before I finally drift off is whether my leaving is going to trigger one of those dozen clauses for Creighton to annul the marriage.

Actually, that's a lie. My very last thought before sleep claims me is how much it would hurt if he did.

CHAPTER
FOUR

Creighton

The penthouse is silent when I let myself inside. I expected to be home almost eight hours ago, but negotiations got heated, and I couldn't step away from the table without losing all the leverage I gained.

If anyone can close a deal with sheer force of will, it's me. Winning this one was too fucking important, and once I had the finish line in sight, I wasn't letting anything get in my way. Although not the biggest dollar deal I've ever done by a long, long shot, I've never had one that meant more on a personal level. Preliminary agreements, including an iron-clad confidentiality agreement, were signed, and I was pretty fucking pleased with myself.

Eager to find Holly, I head for the bedroom, but it's dark. I close in on the bed, looking for the telltale lump that should be curled up dead center, but I find nothing but a smooth comforter.

I flip on the bedside lamp; I'm not sure why exactly. It's not like I can't tell the room is empty, even in the dark.

"Holly?"

Nothing. I flip on every light as I move from room to room.

No Holly. She's not here.

The clothes are here. The guitar is here. But she's not here.

The last time I came home to find the place empty, I flipped the fuck out, thinking she left me. But that was before. The last couple of days, we've . . . well, we've figured some shit out, and what started out as a crazy whim seems like it can actually work.

I also just banked a decent chunk of money on the fact that it can actually work, not that that particular fact matters.

I finally make my way to the kitchen and turn on the lights. A lined piece of notebook paper sits in the center of the island counter.

Two words.

Just two fucking words.

Good-bye, Creighton.

"You've got to be fucking kidding me," I roar. "No fucking way!"

Last time I thought she left me, and I was wrong. This time, I'm not sure how I can be wrong when it's as plain as the ink on the goddamn page. The Amex Black Card I gave her is right beside it. That sends a whole message of its own.

"Fuck me. No fucking way." I don't know why I'm talking to the empty room, but I can't seem to stop myself. "She doesn't get to leave me. I'm not fucking done with her."

I grab my phone and find her number. I hit Send. It goes straight to voice mail.

I call over and over and over until I'm just staring at the phone and getting more and more pissed every time her voice mail picks up.

"This is Holly. You know what to do."

I'm not sure how many times I've called her when I finally leave a message.

"Holly, this is your fucking husband. Where the fuck are you? And if you think you're fucking done with me, you're dead wrong, sweetheart. Better get ready, because I'm fucking coming for you."

An absent thought about winning an award for the number of times I'd used variations on the word *fuck* floats through my brain as I hang up and call Cannon.

"Dude, the deal is inked. You better not have cold feet now," he says rather than *hello*.

"She's gone," I say without preamble.

"Come again?"

"She's fucking gone. Left a note that said good-bye. She's *fucking gone*."

"Shit. Maybe we can undo the deal."

"That's not why I'm calling. It's only money. What I

23

Meghan March

want is my fucking wife back. So go find her."

Cannon clears his throat. "Um, she called. This afternoon, but I knew you didn't want to be disturbed."

Unable to believe what I just heard, I still. "Please repeat yourself."

"She called. I told her you were busy."

"And what did she say?" I bite out each word.

"Nothing. She just . . . hung up." In the background, I hear Cannon typing furiously. "I'll get our guy on it. I'll check her credit cards."

My brain, exhausted from hours at the negotiating table playing mind games with the other side, shifts into gear again. "You're going to have to track her personal credit cards, because she left the one I gave her."

"Damn, man. That's harsh. Or maybe nice? Fuck, I don't know. At least she didn't go out and spend a shit-ton of money and leave you with the bill."

"Considering she left every other goddamn thing— the clothes, the shoes, the fucking guitar—I'm not surprised." The fact that she left the guitar grates the most. It's a giant fuck-you, if I've ever seen one.

The guitar is what trips my memory. *Fuuuuck.*

I fucked up. Her tour; she had to be there. I didn't even think. She has no idea what I did for her . . . and she fucking left.

"I'll call you back when I've got something," Cannon says.

"No need. She's gone back to Nashville. Get the jet online. I want to be in the air in an hour. Make sure I've got a car waiting on the tarmac, and text me her fucking

24

address."

The last part is a little humbling to add, considering I should probably know my wife's address for her last residence. But I also didn't care enough to ask before. Because I was more than content to have her in my bed, in my fucking penthouse, and not ask many questions about her life before me. That was apparently a big fucking mistake.

"Will do, man. Hold up—the jet is already ready to go. Captain Jim is on standby."

Of course it fucking is. Because I *forgot*. I dig a finger and a thumb into my temples and close my eyes.

"Tell the captain I'll be right there."

"Will do."

I hang up and head for the bedroom. All the clothes I instructed a personal shopper to pick out for Holly mock me as I fill my suitcase. I don't know what the fuck I'm supposed to pack for groveling, and I sure as hell haven't ever been to a country concert, but I'm fresh out of flannel shirts and cowboy boots. So I toss in some jeans, T-shirts, a few suits—because you never know when you might need one—and all the rest of my shit.

I'm out the door in less than ten minutes. I'm going to find my wife.

In Nashville, dawn is still a couple of hours away when I park the rented Mercedes SL65 AMG at the curb of an apartment building that has seen better days.

This is where Holly lives?

My anger at her record label grows exponentially. They've been making plenty of money off her, and yet she's been paid practically nothing for her work. Motherfuckers. That's going to end in short order.

I make my way up the crumbling sidewalk to the cracked stoop and scan the list of names by the door. Before I press the buzzer, someone exits and holds the door open for me, so I'm able to head right upstairs—because the security is fucking nonexistent.

Wickman is listed as being on the fourth floor, apartment E, and there's a sign taped to the elevator that reads Out of Order in faded black marker. I can only guess how long it's been there. One thing is for damn sure—Holly won't be staying another night in this dump.

I climb the steps three at a time and knock. It's the closest approximation I can get to *polite* at this point.

I wait.

No answer.

I knock again. Less politely.

No answer, so I bang on the door.

"Holly, open the fucking door."

The door across the hall creaks open, and I turn to see a blond guy with dreads sticking his head out.

"Dude, keep it the fuck down. Some of us are trying to sleep."

I ignore him and continue banging on the door.

"She ain't here, man. And I don't think she's coming back for a while."

According to the tour schedule Cannon e-mailed me, they weren't scheduled to be in Dallas until the night after tomorrow.

I turn back to the stoner. "How do you know she isn't here? And how the fuck do you know she's not coming back for a while?"

"Calm down, bro. I saw her carry a suitcase out last night."

I don't ask why he was watching Holly carry a suitcase out because it doesn't matter. She's never coming back to this place, and she'll never see him again.

I call Cannon when I hit the curb. "She's already gone. Find out where that tour stops next."

"On it."

"Now. While I'm on the goddamn phone."

"Said I'm on it, Crey. Hold on, I got something. Looks like there's a new stop on the tour."

I climb into the Mercedes and haul ass back to the jet.

CHAPTER FIVE

Creighton

"**Y**ou've got to be fucking kidding me," I say to the security guard standing between me and the entrance to the backstage area of the Majestic Theatre in San Antonio.

"No one gets back here without a pass, and you ain't got a pass."

"My wife is back there."

"Don't fucking care, man. You ain't got a pass. You call her and you get her to give you a pass, then you can go back there."

Considering Holly still hasn't answered a single one of my calls, I'm not about to admit that isn't a possibility. I've spent all day in San Antonio trying to track her down, and my patience is shot. The theatre lights go dark.

"Show's startin', man. Get your seat before I have you escorted out."

I open my mouth to argue, but a spotlight snaps on, illuminating the stage, and a very round man dressed in a radio station T-shirt strolls out with a microphone.

"Are ya'll ready for this little lady?"

The crowd yells back, but apparently their response isn't sufficient for his purpose.

"I said, *are ya'll ready for Holly Wix*?"

The crowd roars, and I decide the security guy's suggestion isn't a bad one. I might as well find my seat, because it seems I've finally found my wife.

I had to buy a ticket from a scalper out front because the show was sold out. On the upside, my seat's in the second row, so I'm not going to complain. Leaving the security guard behind, I slide down the row to my designated seat to find three screaming teenage girls on one side of me, and a middle-aged woman who is not at all excited on the other.

I ignore all of them as the announcer says, "Then give a warm San Antonio welcome to Ms. Holly Wix!"

The spotlight goes dark for a moment, and a drummer starts with a beat. One guitar joins in, and then a second, and the stage lights come up.

And there she is.

My fucking wife.

She's wearing a tiny black leather skirt, over-the-knee silver leather boots with fringe, and a tight silver halter top. Her hair is bigger than I've ever seen it, and a ton of glittery makeup has her looking every inch the country starlet.

"Hey, San Antonio! Ya'll are lookin' gorgeous tonight."

Her accent is thicker than I've ever heard it. It rarely slips out when she's around me, and I wonder if she tries to hide it. I don't like the idea of my wife hiding anything.

My thoughts are drowned out of my brain when the teenage girls next to me start screaming in the highest pitch humans can probably register. I catch phrases like, "Holly, we love you!" and "Holly, you're so awesome!"

For a moment I wonder if Holly was like those girls in her younger years. Going to concerts and dreaming about standing on a stage like this, and playing for a crowd.

"Love you too, girls!" Holly calls out before launching into an upbeat song.

It's one that even I recognize because it's the music on a commercial that has been airing for months. Most of the crowd rise to their feet, many singing along with her.

I stay seated, soaking up the woman onstage in front of me.

I've heard her sing in the shower, and compared to this it was like listening to Beethoven plink out a master-piece on a child's toy piano—absolutely no comparison.

Holly's incredibly fucking talented.

And she's mine.

The crowd loves her—including the guy with the sign that says Marry Me, Holly.

She can't fucking marry you, douchebag. She's already married to me.

Right then, I realize I'm jealous. For the first time in my life, I'm fucking *jealous*. And it's of a teenage boy hold-

30

ing a piece of hot pink fucking poster board.

I don't get jealous. Ever. It's an uncomfortable feeling, and I don't like it.

Holly plays only five songs before thanking the crowd and waving as she leaves the stage.

I could have listened to her—watched her—all night. Her sweet twang sank its claws into me, and those sassy lyrics were made all that much sassier by her red lips and swinging hips.

I think I've just become a country music fan. Cannon will never let me hear the end of it.

As soon as the theatre lights come up between acts, I'm out of my seat and heading for the security guy. I've got my wallet out and two grand in my hand when I stop in front of him.

"Not again," he mumbles. "Dude, step off."

"You see that woman who was just onstage?"

He nods as if he's bored with this conversation already.

"She's my fucking wife."

He looks down at my hand. I think he's looking at the money, but his words prove me wrong.

"Where's your ring then?"

I frown. I brought Holly's ring to the hotel room on New Year's Eve. I didn't even consider getting one for myself, and Holly hasn't mentioned it.

Right then I decide that I want Holly to want me to wear a ring. Why the hell hasn't she brought it up before?

"I don't have one. Newlyweds. You might have read about it in the paper. I'm Creighton Karas."

He raises one dark eyebrow. "The billionaire dude?"

"Yeah."

He tilts his head. "Yeah. I guess you could be him."

I flash my license at him. "I *am* him."

"Still ain't letting you backstage without a pass. So put your money away, man."

I grit my teeth, all the muscles in my jaw clenching.

"But you can wait out back by the tour buses after the show. She'll be going out that way, and you can talk to her then. If she wants your ass with her, then she can tell her security to let you on the bus."

I try to hand him the money, but he waves it away. "Nah, man. I'll get fired, and I like my job."

Fair enough. "Thanks for the heads-up."

"Better get yourself a beer and enjoy the rest of the show."

"I'll do that."

And I do.

CHAPTER SIX

Creighton

Four beers and two more acts later, and I'm finally making my way around the back of the theatre to wait. What I find there surprises me. I'm not talking about the heavy metal barricades creating a path for the talent—those don't surprise me. No, it's the half-naked women shoving each other aside to press against those metal barricades. Security is stationed along the way, trying to hold them back, but the women are adamant that they're going to see some guy named Boone or BT or something like that.

I make my way to the edge of a barricade as politely as I can, because I'm not about to shove my way through a bunch of women. But then again, I'm not taking a chance that I'll miss Holly, even if I do feel fucking ridiculous waiting outside with rabid fans like this.

Finally, the back doors open and a swarm of security precedes a crowd of people. The women start screaming, and I'm lifting my hands to plug my ears when I catch sight of Holly.

I call her name, but I don't yell it. She doesn't hear me. Another dozen feet and she'll be standing right in front of me.

Rage burns in me as they get closer and I see the last guy who played—this Boone guy—with his arm around her, holding her against him.

What the fuck?

"Holly." This time it comes out louder and harsher.

The guy drops his arm and comes to the railing a few feet away from me to sign some woman's tits. *Classy guy.* Holly continues toward the bus.

"Holly!"

She jolts to a stop, turns, and her eyes go wide as they lock onto mine. She stumbles, and another man reaches out to steady her. I don't like his hands on her any more than I liked the last guy's arm around her.

Her smile is tight when she comes toward the railing. The tit-signing genius comes down the line, meeting her in front of me.

"You okay, sugar?" he asks her.

Holly opens her mouth to respond, but I beat her to it. "She's fine. She's just wondering why her husband is standing with the groupies."

His eyes cut to me. "So you're the husband, huh?"

"Yeah, I'm the husband."

He looks to Holly. "Didn't mention he was comin.""

"I didn't know he was," she says quietly.

"How about you move this reunion onto the bus?" Boone says.

Holly nods, and he gestures to security. "Get him on my bus. We'll be there in five."

A security guard hops the fence and leads me around the crowd to the tour buses. We slide between the barriers and he raps on the door. It opens, and I climb up the stairs.

It's not the pit I expect it to be. Aside from a case of empty beer cans and a few empty liquor bottles, there's not much garbage. Some clothes, drumsticks, notebooks, guitar picks, and video game controllers litter the counter and table.

I stand next to the couch and wait.

It takes longer than five minutes. Impatient, I move to the tinted windows and watch their slow progression— signing autographs and taking pictures from awkward angles.

Finally, the door opens again, and Holly climbs inside.

I've made myself at home on the couch, and I'm considering what to say. But she beats me to it.

"What are you doing here?" she asks without prelude.

"Looking for my wife," I reply.

She mumbles something in response.

"Excuse me?"

"I said I'm kinda surprised."

My first instinct is to defend myself, but there's really no point. I screwed up, and I know it. That doesn't mean I'm not still pissed that she didn't wait just a little bit longer before she walked out.

I decide an apology is the best choice. It's not my usual, but I'm surprised how easily the words come. "I'm sorry, Holly. I fucked up. I told you I'd be somewhere, and I wasn't."

Her mouth drops open, and I'm instantly reminded of all the things I want to do to that mouth.

A slow clap starts from the front of the bus, interrupting the conversation.

"Now that's a guy who knows how to grovel. I'm taking notes, man, in case I ever get myself up shit creek."

He strolls down the aisle and holds out a hand tattooed with what looks like brass knuckles with skulls. "Boone Thrasher."

I stand and appraise him, man-to-man. "Creighton Karas."

We shake hands, neither trying overly hard to crush the other's, which is more than I expected from a guy with brass knuckles tattooed on his hand. Assumptions and all that.

He's still wearing the ripped jeans, camo ball cap, and biker boots he wore onstage, although he must have pulled on a new T-shirt because he ripped the last one off mid-performance.

"You treat this girl right, you hear? Or you'll answer to me." Thrasher's gaze drills into mine and his words are solemn.

I open my mouth to tell him it's no fucking business of his what I do with Holly, but I pause. Honestly, I'm glad she has someone who cares enough about her to threaten me on her behalf. As long as his concern is completely platonic, we don't have a problem.

"Thanks for the warning. I'm glad Holly has a *friend* at her back."

He catches the emphasis I place on the word friend. "No worries, man. I've got my own woman. Not looking to poach yours." He leans closer and adds, "Besides, if I would've wanted her, you never would've had a shot."

His cocky confidence instantly makes me want to ram my fist into his face, but Holly huffs quietly, apparently over the macho posturing Boone and I are engaging in.

"I'll respectfully disagree with you on that," I reply, ready to end the conversation.

He laughs, a booming sound that fills the bus. I step back and throw a possessive arm around Holly.

Thrasher is smiling when he says, "You just might do, man. Definitely better than that douche, JC." He holds up both hands. "I ain't got no problem with the fact that the man prefers dick to pussy. To each his own. But I do have a problem with him using Holly to pretend that ain't the case. If you're man enough to fuck another man's ass, then you should be man enough to be honest with your fans about it—or at least not demand a beard from the label. Just my opinion. Not that it means shit anyway."

Okay, I just might like this guy.

"That situation has certainly been taken care of."

"Damn straight. I like your style, man."

I nod, more than ready for this conversation to be over. I've got Holly by my side, which means all I want is some time alone with her so we can get some things straight. Namely the fact that she's not ever going to walk out on me again with nothing more than a two-word note. And not walking out on me *period* would be ideal.

"We'll get out of your way. I'm assuming the rest of your band is waiting to get on the bus?"

"They're on the opener bus."

I look to Holly, and she elaborates.

"I'm sharing a bus with the other opening act. The labels split the cost."

I recall the four large bearded lumberjack-looking men who came onstage after Holly, and played a multitude of instruments.

"You share a bus with four men?"

"Seven, if you count the guys in my band too."

"That's over tonight. We'll get a hotel, and I'll deliver you to Dallas."

"I always travel with my band," she protests.

"And now you're traveling with your husband."

Thrasher takes a seat on the couch, not even pretending to give us privacy. In fact, he decides to share his two cents.

"She travels with the tour. That's the way it goes."

"Then she's getting her own bus. Her band can stay with the other group."

He nods approvingly. "That works. Then I can kick their drummer off my bus. But you're going to have to pick up the tab for that. No way the label will."

"Not a concern. If you didn't insist she travel on a bus, I'd arrange for hotels and we'd take the jet."

Thrasher shakes his head and reaches for a bottle of

Johnny Walker Blue Label on the table. At least the man doesn't have bad taste in scotch.

"That's tempting fate, man. Too many good artists have gone down in crashes. I don't hold with that."

"Creighton," Holly says, interrupting us. "We need to talk about this."

I look down at her. "There's nothing to talk about. You need to be here, and I find that I'm unwilling to let you be here without me."

She shakes off my arm, and I drop it from her shoulders. "That's not really your decision to make."

I glance at Thrasher, who may as well go get some popcorn with how raptly he's watching our exchange.

My eyes cut back to Holly. "We're getting a hotel for tonight."

She leans back against the cabinets of the galley kitchen and crosses her arms. I'd be lying if I said I'm not caught on the way her movement pushes her tits up in that halter top.

My eyes are riveted, and I almost miss her words when she says, "We're rolling out of here in a few and driving tonight."

My lips twitch, and I quell the urge to bend her over my knee for her sassy attitude. But that's not something I want an audience for. "What time do you need to be at the venue in the morning?"

Holly lets Thrasher answer. "Long as she's there by noon, you're all good. And if you take your damn jet, just don't tell me. I don't want to know. And I sure as fuck don't want to have to get another opening act if your plane goes down."

I grab Holly's hand and tug her against me. She inhales sharply when she makes contact with my chest. Her hand goes up, and her fingers curl around my shoulder. We need to get the hell out of this bus in a hurry before I forget I don't want a goddamn audience.

I don't look away from her wide brown eyes when I speak. "We'll see you tomorrow at noon, Thrasher."

CHAPTER SEVEN

Holly

Creighton unlocks the hotel suite and holds open the door for me. I find the light switch and wander into the room. Neither of us have spoken since we climbed on the opener bus and Creighton directed me to pack a bag. And when I say directed, I mean ordered.

Throughout this whole exchange, mixed emotions flooded my veins until I was sure they would cause me to burst from the intensity. Shock fought with anger while anger fought with excitement.

I don't know how to feel about this. Happy that he showed up? Or still hurt that he forgot about me? Or pissed that he came in and took over my life?

I couldn't get a lock on any one thing long enough to just *feel* it, let alone put it into words. As always, song lyrics began to float through my head, but like my emotions, they were a jumbled mess.

This is what Creighton does to me, and I'm not sure if I love it or hate it. Isn't there some saying that life begins at the edge of your comfort zone? Well, guess what? I'm living, because I'm so far outside my comfort zone right now, I can't even find the trail back.

These last months were all about trying something new and finding myself, and maybe this is just the next step. I know one thing is certain: I don't want to lose myself to the commanding, overwhelming man that's Creighton Karas. Regardless of what happens next, I need to hold on to the bits and pieces of myself I've fought for, because I matter too. This relationship isn't just about him. If this is going to last beyond the silent ride to the hotel, we need to get clear on that fact.

What did Creighton think when he came back to the penthouse to find it empty? Did he realize he screwed up? Did he go to Nashville first? Is he here to scold me like a child and drag me back by my hair? If that's the case, he's in for some severe disappointment. I'm not leaving this tour.

The swirling possibilities are put to rest when he shuts the door to our room, drops our bags, and growls, "Strip."

My eyes snap to him. This isn't how I expected this scenario to go. "Excuse me?"

"Do I really need to repeat myself?"

"I thought we were going to talk—" I start, but Creighton interrupts.

"I'm done talking. I'm about to show my wife how I

feel about her walking out, not answering her phone, and leaving me to fly to multiple states to track her down."

"You knew—"

He interrupts again. "You left a note with two words, my dear. Two. Fucking. Words. They might as well have been 'Fuck you.'"

"Maybe they should have been," I reply, dumbfounded—and pissed—at his reaction.

"Strip. Now. Or I'll do it for you."

His tone is implacable, and in that moment, I know I can't cave. Maybe it's fitting that I'm in San Antonio, because this might be my frigging Alamo.

I shake my head. "I'm not playing, Creighton."

His expression turns feral. "Did something about this situation make you think I'm *playing*?" He stalks toward me. "You agreed. I call the shots; you follow."

"That deal went out the window when you made it all too clear that you can't be bothered to acknowledge I exist except for when it's convenient for you."

He jerks his head back as if I just slapped him, and stops mid-stride. "Do you really believe that?"

"After yesterday? What else should I believe? You couldn't even be bothered to answer a phone call, and you knew I needed to go!"

"I knew you needed to be in Nashville today. That was the plan. I said I'd get you there last night, but something came up. It happens when you run a multi-billion-dollar company, Holly. That's not going to change."

"I get that. Even little old me understands that, but what I don't get is how you couldn't even take a phone call from me to tell you that plans had changed. I'm on a short leash when it comes to the label. I've got no choice but to follow the rules, or I'm screwed. I told you I'd play by your rules, but when you start putting my career at risk because you can't seem to remember that I have a commitment, that's where my caring about what you want stops."

I fling a hand toward the window and the lights of the Majestic Theatre in the distance. "This is my life. This is my one shot at proving to myself that I'm meant for more than serving up greasy food to bowling teams who argue about who has the biggest beer gut and the biggest man boobs. Do you have any idea how fast this could all fall apart for me? Then I'd be right back where I started, and I *refuse* to let that happen just because I didn't give this absolutely everything I've got."

"And what makes you think I'd let that happen? That's not something you need to worry about anymore." Creighton's frustration is clear in his tone, but he still doesn't get it.

"Bull. Your prenup makes it damn clear that I still can't count on anyone but myself. Besides, I didn't come this far on my own to start depending on a guy to take care of me now."

Creighton's head tilts to the side. "Holly—"

I swing my head back to face him. "No. You don't understand. Once you put my future on the line, this stops being a game."

His brow furrows and his features tighten. "I'm well aware this isn't a game. And I'm also well aware that I'm the one who fucked up by losing track of your schedule.

But that doesn't mean I don't need to put us back on an even keel the only way I know how."

I assume he's talking about sex, because that seems to be the only part of this marriage where we're compatible. But still, that doesn't mean I have to like his methods.

I stride into the bedroom and sit on the edge of the bed, unzipping my right boot before tossing it across the room. Creighton crosses the threshold, and it flies perilously close to his head. It wasn't my intention, at least not a conscious one. The second boot follows. He says nothing as it whizzes by his left side. A quick glance at his face reveals a crooked smirk. I tug off my boot socks and reach for the zipper on my skirt.

His voice is quieter this time. "Holly, what are you doing?"

"Following orders. What does it look like?"

I shove the skirt and my underwear down over my hips and tug my top over my head. Each article of clothing lands at his feet as I toss them.

I rip the duvet off the king-sized bed and climb up into the middle. I flip onto my back and spread my legs wide.

"Is that good enough for you? Is that *stripped* enough for you?"

Creighton closes in on the bed. "Are you going to explain this, or am I going to have to guess what you're trying to accomplish with this stunt?"

"No stunt. I'm just following orders."

Creighton's lips twitch into a wolfish grin. "Oh, Holly, you know how to tempt me, that's not in doubt. But I don't think this is going to work out quite how you're thinking."

I cock my head sideways on the fluffy pillow. "Really? I submit, you fuck me, I come, you come, and then maybe we repeat."

He tosses the duvet up and over me.

Okay, apparently I'm wrong.

"You make me sound so predictable, my lovely wife, and I can't have that."

He circles the bed, sits on the edge with his back to me, and lifts the cordless phone from the receiver.

"Room service, thank you." Once he's connected, he says, "A porterhouse and a filet. Medium rare. Two Caesar salads." He rattles off the name of something I assume is an expensive wine, thanks the individual on the other end, and hangs up.

I crush the duvet to my chest and sit up. "What the hell just happened?"

Creighton stands and turns to me. "I decided I'm having your pussy for dessert rather than as an appetizer."

Once again, my mind spins. "I repeat, what the hell just happened?"

Creighton ignores my second question and crosses the room to the closet. He unrolls the sleeves of his white dress shirt, shrugs it off, and hangs it up.

"Holy shit, he's wearing jeans. How is it possible that I missed that?" I mumble to myself. But apparently my mumble isn't quiet enough to escape Creighton's ears.

"Probably the screaming fans, poorly lit bus, and your plotting to rip me a new asshole."

"I didn't know you owned jeans."

"You would have if you'd actually stepped foot in the closet where the clothes I bought you were hanging."

I stiffen, my fingers tensing against the fluffy down. "I didn't need all that. Any of it."

"Even the guitar?" he asks, his dark gaze landing on me.

I hate how he drives right to the heart of things when I don't want to discuss them.

"I thanked you for the guitar."

"And yet you left it. I'm assuming that was a personal statement rather than a practical one."

I refuse to break his stare. "You already bought me once, Karas. You don't need to keep trying to buy me."

"The guitar is on the jet."

My heart clenches. I loved that glittery turquoise Gibson. Really, really loved it.

I'm still trying to decide how to respond when Creighton says, "Do you want to shower before dinner? It should be here shortly."

I think about the ten pounds of stage makeup I'm still wearing, and stand. I'm almost surprised that he phrased it as a question, but I don't hesitate before climbing off the bed and going to my bag for my toiletry case.

I take my time in the shower, replaying what just happened and trying to figure out this man I'm married to. Spoiler—I fail. He's impossible to predict, and I think I'm going to drive myself crazy trying. I don't exit the bathroom until I hear the outer door open and shut.

Shrugging on a fluffy robe from the bathroom, I peek my head around the door frame and see a man unloading domed dishes from a cart and setting up our meal at the table.

Memories of our sushi dinner once again filter into my brain. Given how tonight has gone, I can safely say we won't be sitting on top of the table eating our steaks. But considering how long it's been since I've had steak, I'm good with sitting properly and devouring it. I tell myself that I deserve it. One night off the *Holly needs to stay skinny on tour so she's visually appealing* diet won't kill me.

The man lifts the covers, uncorks the wine, and offers further service, but Creighton thanks him and sends him on his way. I don't leave my shadow-darkened post at the bedroom doorway until I hear the outer door close.

When I step out into the living room, I find Creighton pouring me a glass of wine. The protest on my lips dies when I inhale the rich aroma of the meal. I get that lots of people have moral or other objections to eating meat, and I respect that, but I'm a Kentucky girl who loves a good steak.

Creighton pulls out my chair, and I sink into my seat. *Is this his way of trying to make amends?* If he just wanted sex from me, he could have taken me up on my offer. So maybe I play this cool and see how it goes?

I hate needing a strategy, but with Creighton I feel like I need to be ready for anything. *How about just be normal, Holly?* But what's our normal? I decide to just be me. The nice version, not the one who throws shoes at a guy's head.

"That smells amazing."

"Glad you approve."

I smile. "I might not even complain about you ordering for me because you rocked it like a rodeo cowboy. But rest assured," I say as I pick up my fork and steak knife, "the first time you order pâté or caviar and expect me to eat it and like it, your meal-selection privileges will get yanked faster than a weed from my gran's garden."

"Duly noted."

I flick my gaze up to Creighton's for only a moment before I cut into the filet. Lifting it to my mouth, I pop it inside and groan appreciatively as I chew. Other than the meal at Johnny Utah's, this is the first time I've really indulged.

After I swallow, I mumble, "Fourteen months without red meat. Should be a crime."

Creighton catches my comment. "Why would you go fourteen months without red meat if you clearly enjoy it so much?"

I'm too focused on the delicious meal to give him anything but an absent account of the absolute truth. "Before the show, I was living on PB&J and ramen, putting every spare cent toward my gran's medical bills. And during and after, it was on the *don't you dare think about putting that in your mouth* list."

Creighton lifts his glass and takes a sip of wine. "Then I'm glad you're having it tonight. Tell me about—"

I interrupt what I'm sure will be a question about Gran. I may have brought her up, but I don't want to talk about her. I've already bared my body tonight; I don't think I can handle baring my soul.

"Just don't tell my manager or the costume people. They'll get out the pitchforks. I'm not allowed to gain weight. Actually, I'm supposed to lose another ten pounds before the ACM Awards. But I hate exercise, and after tasting steak again, I'm not sure how I can go back to chicken and steamed vegetables."

Creighton's fork clatters against the china. "That's fucking ridiculous. I forbid it."

Cue my *What the hell did you just say?* look.

"Um, excuse me, but it's not your place to forbid anything," I reply, losing the *nice Holly* attitude.

"You lose another pound, and I will ensure it's the last pound you lose."

Well. That sounds ominous.

"And it's still not your place to make that kind of call."

"Holly—"

"Creighton—"

We both lapse into stubborn silence for a few moments, and I drop my attention back to my plate. He does the same, and I wonder if he's going to drop the issue. Then I take another bite of my steak and forget to care.

I'm almost finished with my dinner when Creighton's cell rings. He pulls it from the pocket of his jeans and apologizes.

"I have to take this."

He leaves the room, and I can't hear much of his side of the conversation except for a few comments like "that motherfucker" and "we'll never concede." Neither of those two sentiments indicate he's enjoying the phone call.

While he's gone, I polish off the rest of my steak and salad, and one of those jumbled song lyrics from earlier starts nagging at me. I'm at the desk, scribbling away on a pad of paper, when Creighton returns.

His hair is sticking up in the front, as if he's been jamming his fingers into it over and over. Just one more sign it wasn't a good phone call.

This is where a real wife stops what she's doing and asks what's wrong. I finish off the lyric and decide to give that wife thing a try.

"What's up?" Okay, admittedly it's not the most brilliant of conversation starters, but it's open ended, and I'm inviting him to share what all the cursing was about.

"Nothing you need to worry about."

And there it is—the difference between this marriage and one where the spouses are *actually* trying to make a connection. Something about it breaks a little piece inside me. A piece of what, I refuse to speculate.

"Oh, you don't say. Darling, that's awful. I wish there was something I could do to help." My babbling, batshit-crazy response earns me a sharp look from Creighton. "What? I'm trying to pretend that I'm a wife whose husband actually just shared something in his life, and I give a crap."

His look, if possible, gets sharper. But it's his words that surprise me the most. "You really want to know?"

"Lay it on me, hubs. I'm living dangerously tonight," I drawl, letting my accent loose.

Creighton crosses the room to the desk and leans against it so he's facing me, his thigh only inches from my arm. Which means his dick is probably only a foot from my mouth, and I can't help but think about dessert.

I tear my eyes away from his package, which is displayed rather prominently in his jeans, and meet his dark brown stare—a stare that's still narrowed on me. He's taking my measure, gauging my actual interest in what he's dealing with.

I decide to make it easy for him. "All sass aside, I really am here if you want to talk about what's going on."

Something flashes through his expression, but before I can pin it down, it's gone.

"That was Cannon."

"Okay," I say, prompting him to continue.

"We have an activist shareholder causing trouble. He's getting the street wound up about the company's business strategy, and he's demanding changes as well as additional independent directors on the board to balance the decision-making."

I'm following him, but most of this means nothing to me.

"What exactly is an activist shareholder?"

"Someone with enough of a stake in the company that we have to take him seriously when he makes a big public stink. It's an inflammatory way of trying to effect change in the way the company does business."

"Okay." I consider his explanation for a beat. "Isn't that kind of par for the course in your business?"

He nods. "Yes, but in this case it's even more of a nuisance because the activist shareholder is also my uncle."

My eyebrows shoot up. "Your uncle?"

His smile is grim. "Yes. The uncle who was responsible for my upbringing from the age of ten to eighteen."

I like words, mostly because I like to twist them

into songs that convey some kind of emotional reaction. Creighton, I've come to notice, chooses his words carefully. He didn't just say *the uncle who raised me*.

"I'm assuming you're not close."

"You'd assume right. He made his money in the foreign currency exchange markets, and then got an ego boost when I did the same thing—regardless of the fact that he didn't teach me a damn thing himself. Once I took my company public, he decided he wanted a big enough piece of it to piss me off."

"It sounds like your relationship is . . . complicated."

A muscle in Creighton's jaw ticks. "You could say that."

"So, is this the kind of trouble that's just annoying? Or is it serious?"

Creighton shifts, crossing his arms over his chest. "In all honesty, I'm not entirely certain yet. Up until now, he's just been a nuisance—demanding that I start selling off some of the businesses the company owns, which is something I refuse to do to silence him. But now, suffice it to say he's trying alternative tactics."

Once again, I dissect Creighton's words carefully. What he isn't saying is coming through just as strongly.

"Do these alternative tactics have something to do with me, or us getting married?"

Creighton's chest lifts and falls on a breath. "He's finding some ammunition in that, yes."

I'm actually surprised by his candid answer. I expected him to dodge the question altogether.

"Is there anything I can do to help?"

Unlike a few minutes earlier, I'm not being sassy in the

slightest. If there's something I can do to help, I will—and not just because Creighton's name being dragged through the mud now means that my name is being muddied as well.

"I'll figure it out." He looks at me. "But thanks."

I start to shrug but it turns into a yawn. "Just holler if there's anything you think of."

Creighton studies me. "You're tired."

It's not a question, but I reply anyway. "Yeah, first show after a break. It's easy to forget how exhausting it is. Not to mention the rehearsal, sound check, meet and greet, and everything else."

"Then I guess you should call it a night."

"I need to be in Dallas by noon for a radio interview. I hope that's not an issue."

He shakes his head slowly. "Not an issue. It's a quick flight. We'll be there in plenty of time."

"Okay then." I push the chair back from the desk and stand, tugging the belt of the robe tighter and staring at my silver-polished toenails. I glance up at Creighton. "I guess I'll just be going to bed."

I take a hesitant step toward the bedroom, waiting for him to grab me by the belt, yank me against his chest, and growl something about me forgetting about his dessert.

But he does none of those things. Instead, I'm treated to an absent nod.

"I'll try not to disturb you. I've got a few hours' worth of work ahead of me."

Really, Creighton? Really? After your orders to strip earlier? I give him a moment to change his mind. He doesn't.

Okay, then.

"No problem. I sleep like the dead. Nothing wakes me. Comes from three months of sleeping on a bus with a bunch of snoring men."

Creighton's features tense, obliterating his previously relaxed expression. "That's changing tomorrow too. Your new bus will be waiting after the concert."

My mouth starts moving before my mind can tell it to shut up. "That'll be great. I won't have to worry about keeping my orgasms silent anymore."

The corners of Creighton's mouth curl into a crooked smirk. He pushes off the desk and closes the distance between us.

"No, Holly, that certainly won't be an issue anymore. In fact, I'll have a hell of a problem if you aren't moaning for me tomorrow night on that bus."

I can't keep up with the man's moods, but it's the smirk that does me in. I shiver at his words as they whisper over me. My hand, which seemingly develops a will of its own, reaches for the button of his jeans.

And . . . his fucking cell rings again.

I drop my hand. "I guess that means I'm going to bed alone, then."

He reaches for his phone, checking the screen. "If I didn't have to take this call . . ."

I shrug. "I could use the extra sleep anyway. They'll want to do photos at the radio station, so I need to look like I could pass as a chart-topper."

Creighton slides his finger across the screen of his phone, and I turn away.

"Hold on a minute, please."

I pause, not knowing if he's speaking to me or the person on the phone. Peeking over my shoulder, I see him slide the phone onto the desk and step toward me. He tucks his hand in the belt of my robe and tugs me toward him in the exact move I envisioned only minutes ago.

"I'm taking a rain check on my dessert," he says, and slants his mouth over mine.

I open to him and his tongue delves inside, tasting my mouth so deliciously that my thighs squeeze together, and I can feel the slickness growing between my legs. Cupping the back of my head, he grips my hair and tilts me the opposite direction, not wasting a breath as the kiss deepens and intensifies. I'm lost in the moment when he releases his grip on me.

Standing in stunned silence, I stare as he picks up his phone, unmutes it, leans back against the desk, and begins speaking.

"Give it to me," he says into the phone, but I feel like his words are directed at me.

A small smile forms on my lips, and I reach for the belt of my robe and slowly untie it. I let the plush terrycloth fall open and lift my hand to rest between my breasts.

I'm not sure what little devil is guiding me, but I'm sure one must be.

Creighton's eyes zero in on my hands as he listens—or attempts to listen—to whoever is on the other end of the call.

Now that I have his attention, I skim my fingers down my body until they spread and cover my pussy. Just thinking the word always makes me hotter.

His dark eyes burn into me, and I can tell he's stopped even attempting to listen to a damn thing that's being said. I love that I have the power to distract him like this, even as I wonder what the heck I'm doing. It's as if I need to prove to myself that I have something he wants. Maybe I'm seeking some kind of validation?

I don't question what I'm feeling. I just go with it.

I dip two fingers between my lips and swirl them in the wetness that has gathered. A push of my wrist, and I slip both fingers inside me. Moaning, I let my eyes flutter shut for a beat before sliding my fingers in and out.

Oh. Lord.

I open my eyes again—just in time to see Creighton's lips form a single silent word.

"Fuck."

My smile feels lazy and seductive as I continue to tease myself. I slide my fingers up, flicking my clit and sending a jolt of pleasure through myself. I think for a second about just making myself come, but decide to savor the anticipation and lift my hand away.

I step toward Creighton.

Reaching my fingertips to his full lips, I paint them with my wetness. His tongue darts out to lick, grabbing my wrist with both hands and sucking my fingers into his mouth.

After he's drawn every bit of slickness from my skin, he releases my fingers and growls into the phone, "I'll call you back."

He drops the phone to the carpet, and his feral expression turns on me. "That was the hottest fucking thing I've ever seen in my life."

I smile, the flush of victory heating my cheeks. I stunned him. Who knew that could happen?

And then he says, "You're going to go bend over the end of the bed, spread your legs, and I'm going to spank that tight little ass and your naughty little cunt before I fuck you so hard, you'll still be feeling me tomorrow when you step onstage."

The flush of heat spreads to my chest, my nipples pucker painfully tight, and my inner muscles clench.

Stunned?

I guess it's my turn.

CHAPTER
EIGHT

Creighton

I prowl after Holly as she turns and heads for the bedroom. My cock pulses against my zipper, and if Cannon faults me for hanging up on him, he can go straight to hell.

Because I've just learned a valuable lesson—there *is* something more important than business, and she's letting the white terrycloth robe dip across her back as it slides down her arms, revealing the most perfect ass I've ever had the pleasure of seeing.

I planned to go slow. To tease her. To savor this. To watch her follow my instructions to the letter. But instead, I surge forward and cup her ass in both hands. She's standing in front of the bed, and I push her forward until she's bent over it.

"You have no idea how badly I just want to slide inside

this perfect ass." My lips skim her ear, and she shivers.

"Do it," she whispers.

A smile stretches across my face. "Oh, Holly, haven't you figured out yet that you don't get to give the orders here? Don't you remember the rules?"

She shoves her ass back, as if trying to tempt me to stray from my plan.

"You know you want to," she says, louder this time.

I step back, releasing my hold on her. "I think I've been too lax in making sure you understand who calls the shots here. You've more than earned your punishment, you dirty girl, and I'm going to enjoy the hell out of giving it to you."

She turns her head to the side, her cheek resting on the crisp white sheets. Her brown eyes spark with challenge, and a pink flush of arousal colors her cheekbone and neck. I want to see that pink blush on her ass.

My hand swings and connects under the curve of her right cheek with a sharp smack. Holly inhales sharply and moans, her hips pressing into the bed.

I land another strike in the same place on the opposite side, and her moan grows louder. My handprint blooms reddish-pink on her skin, and this time I groan.

"Goddamn. You look so fucking sexy with my marks on you. Get up on the bed. On your knees. Now."

She doesn't hesitate, but complies immediately. I'll reward her for that . . . soon. But right now, I need to give her more of this.

I pepper her skin with smack after smack. Her back is arched, ass thrusting up at me as if begging for more.

I slip my hand between her legs and stroke.

"So fucking wet, baby. Give me your hand."

She turns her head to look back at me, confusion creasing her forehead.

"You're going to finger-fuck that tight little pussy while I watch because I want a replay of that sexy-as-fuck show you put on for me. If you thought you were just going to tease me, you were wrong. I'm going to stroke my cock until I finish between those perfect lips of yours, and then you're going to take me down your throat until I'm hard enough to fuck your naughty cunt."

Her mouth drops open and my dick surges, wanting inside that hot, wet heaven.

"I haven't had nearly enough of that dirty little mouth of yours. Now put that hand on your pussy and show me how you make yourself come."

She lets out a breathy, "Oh my God," before she faces forward once more and follows my instructions. I cup her ass and give her one more sharp slap for her delay before reaching for the button of my jeans.

I don't even have my zipper down yet, and her fingers are buried inside her pussy. Gripping my dick, I squeeze it tight. But the moans and whimpers and bobbing of Holly's ass have precum already dripping from the tip. I reach between her legs and pull her hand away.

"I need some of this." Dipping my hand into her wetness, I coat my palm before telling her to continue. I start to stroke, my precum and Holly's slickness easing each slide of my hand.

"You're such a dirty fucking girl," I tell her as I see one

of her fingers ease out of her pussy and skim the pucker of her ass. "You need something filling your ass to help you come faster, baby?"

She nods.

"Give me the words, Holly."

"Please," she whispers.

"You're not ready for my cock yet."

She shakes her head.

"Show me what you want, Holly."

Her curious little finger rims her ass, but doesn't slip inside.

She looks back at me, teeth sinking into her bottom lip. "Please."

Holly looks like she's teetering on the edge of orgasm, desperate for the little push that will send her over. I may not have packed much, but I remembered to pack the important stuff.

"Don't move."

I turn and head for my bag. After wiping off my hand, I retrieve the plug and lube in record time. I've got the package open and the silicone coated liberally when I step back into the bedroom.

The sight of Holly on her knees, ass in the air and her hand between her legs, nearly has me coming on the spot.

Fuck me, but this woman is perfect.

CHAPTER
NINE

Holly

Creighton stops at the end of the bed and holds up a hot pink butt plug. It's definitely bigger than the last one we used, but right now, I don't care. I'm reaching for what might be the most intense orgasm of my life, and I'm beyond caring about anything. I'm begging for him to shove something up my ass, and I know I should feel embarrassed or ashamed, but all I care about is the mind-blowing pleasure I know will follow.

"Fucking perfect." Or at least I think that's what he whispers when he lowers his head and presses a kiss to the base of my spine, and then one to each dimple at the top of my ass.

My nipples pucker as he slides the tip of the plug down my crack until it's resting against my ass. The slick trail of lube tells me he's already prepared it for me. The pressure is exquisite as he presses it forward just a smidge at a time. I arch my back, shoving back against it, and inhale sharply at the burn.

He backs off immediately, and his palm slaps the outside of my thigh. "Slow down, baby. You'll get what I give you, and you'll like it."

He's already started nudging the plug back inside me, and my fingers work my clit faster and faster. I can feel my arousal dripping down my hand, and I'm nearly mindless with pleasure when he's stretched me and seated the plug.

The same palm that slapped me before now caresses my ass, and I push back into it.

"Fucking beautiful," he says, and in that moment, I feel beautiful. I feel . . .

My thoughts shut down as the orgasm solidifies and shatters inside me. I think I moan his name, but I have no idea.

I drop my hand, ready to ride out the pleasure as it subsides, but Creighton has other ideas. His fingers take over, pinching my clit and stealing another orgasm from me.

"Oh. My. God," I whisper, my eyes slamming shut as the arm I'm using to hold myself up shakes and my elbows give way.

Creighton catches me before I land face-first on the bed. He lifts me back up onto my knees, but doesn't stop until my back is against him. His fingers disappear, but then I feel the head of his cock against my pussy.

"I'm taking a rain check on fucking that mouth of

yours. Right now, I need to be inside you." He thrusts, seating himself to the base with one ruthless push.

The plug in my ass makes him seem twice as big, and the stretch of his cock sends my body into pleasure overload.

"Creighton!" Another orgasm rips through me, but he doesn't slow. He holds me pinned to him with an arm under my breasts as he thrusts into me over and over.

I can feel his breath as he speaks against my ear. "One more time. I'm not stopping until I feel that perfect cunt of yours strangle my cock *one more time*." His lips slide across my shoulder just before his teeth press against my skin.

I don't know if it's his words, his teeth, or my own hand between my legs, but in that moment, I detonate.

CHAPTER
TEN

Creighton

Having a wife was supposed to be convenient, and when I woke up this morning with my cock between my wife's lips, it was incredibly fucking convenient.

But now? Now I'm starting to realize there is nothing convenient about being married to Holly Wickman Karas, and yet there's nothing that could drag me away from her. Not even the fact that my uncle is causing trouble and riling up Wall Street. If there was ever a time I should be at the helm, showing the world that the company I've built from nothing is the center of my life, it's now.

But I'm not at my desk. I'm in Dallas, still living in Holly's world, and trying to figure out how one formerly innocent country girl claimed that center spot.

Everything I feel about her is unsettling, and I'm not

ready to fucking talk about any of it. So instead, I focus on the here and now, and leave the complicated little fuckers called emotions to another day.

The woman is a workhorse—and I mean that in the most complimentary way imaginable. A trophy wife, she is not. She slipped on a pair of headphones the moment we climbed on the jet this morning, and pulled out a notebook. She was already scribbling away before takeoff. She waved off breakfast, barely looking up until we landed and I stood next to her, holding out a hand. I've never spent much time around creative types—all of my acquaintances tend to be like me—so this has been an education.

On the drive from the airport, I practically had to shove food in her mouth to get her to eat, as she seemed content to bob her head, hum, and scribble. She didn't come out of her writing zone until we pulled up to the radio station, where she hopped out of the car, and I had to jog to catch up.

After a radio interview, dozens of autographs, pictures, and off-air questions, she headed back to the car. I began to feel like a chauffeur when she slipped her headphones back on and said, "We're going to the venue next, right?" She didn't wait for an answer before picking up her pen and starting to scribble again.

I couldn't get her attention until we arrived at the venue. Well, to be fair, it wasn't me that got her attention, but the giant new luxury coach I arranged to be delivered. And it didn't actually catch her attention until she started to walk by it and I snagged her hand.

"This one's yours."

She stared up at the gleaming black-and-silver coach, eyes blinking. "No friggin' way."

I smiled at her unvarnished response. "Yes friggin' way."

My visions of christening the coach in style were obliterated when the members of her band climbed off the other bus, and she became all business. I was curious to watch their rehearsal, but a conference call had me climbing on Holly's new bus and firing up my laptop. Alone. And I thought this marriage was going to be fucking convenient.

By the time I've finished up work, Holly still hasn't returned. A look at the clock says it's now almost six.

Shit.

Did I miss it?

Fuck.

I flip my laptop shut and hurry off the bus, flashing the pass that some skinny guy dropped off about three hours ago. Something about all-access. At least tonight I won't be trying to bribe some security guard the size of a giant to get backstage. That's a marginal improvement.

I find someone who looks like she knows what the hell is going on, and after her eyes practically bug out of her head when she realizes who I am, she points me in the direction of Holly's dressing room.

My knock on the door is answered with a simple "come in," and I throw the door wide open.

Holly is surrounded by three people—a man going after her face with what look like makeup brushes and sponges, another man messing with her hair, and a woman running a lint roller across an outfit hanging from a hook on the wall. They're fussing and clucking and doing God knows what.

They don't pause when I enter, so I find myself a chair in the corner and settle in to check the e-mails that keep buzzing on my phone. A few other people continuously bang in and out of the room, tossing out bits of information that don't catch my attention. I slip into my own little world, in a corner of Holly's world, until Holly stands and undoes the top buttons on her plaid shirt.

I stand, *calmly*, and cross the room to pause in front of her chair.

"A moment, if you would," I say. Again, *calmly*. And then I back her into a corner of the room behind a screen.

Her eyebrows are bunched together in confusion. "What's wrong?" she asks, glancing beyond the screen and back at me.

"What the fuck do you think you're doing?" I growl from between clenched teeth.

"Changing." Her slow, measured response suggests I'm a dumb fuck.

"Not in front of a roomful of people, you're not."

I jab a hand in the general direction of the door, which even now, I can hear opening and closing with what seems like more traffic than a damn freeway.

With a flip of her now wavy hair, Holly brushes off my concern and presses a hand to my chest in an attempt to shove me out of the way so she can get out from behind the screen.

When I don't budge, she says, "Creighton, everyone in this room has seen me mostly naked dozens of times."

An insane thought fires through my brain, and I shove it away. I shouldn't be wondering if any of my companies have access to technology to create memory loss in humans. If she were any other woman, I wouldn't care if the whole world saw her naked.

But this woman? I do. I very much do. Why? Doesn't matter beyond the fact that *she's my fucking wife.*

A caveman didn't need to understand the urge to drag a woman back to his cave where the other cave assholes can't see her perfect fucking body. This is a physiological reaction, millennia in the making, over which I have zero control. The rationalization makes my intense possessiveness easier to swallow.

"I don't give a damn if every person in the entire fucking stadium saw you buck-ass naked before. You're Mrs. Creighton Karas now. The rules have changed."

The word "rules" brings color to her face, and I wonder if she's thinking of last night when I asked her if she remembered the rule about me being in charge.

Turns out I'm wondering *wrongly.*

The hands pressing against my chest pull back and slam palm-first into my pecs. Unprepared for her shove, I stumble back a step and into the screen, scraping it across the floor.

"What the hell, Holly?"

"You're such an *asshole*!" She whisper-yells this at me, but the chatter in the room goes silent.

I stick my head out from behind the screen and announce, "Everyone out."

The woman eyeballs me and looks like she's going to

argue, but she just says, "You've got ten minutes. And then she needs to get changed. We've got a meet and greet to do."

Considering I dislike being told what to do on the best of days, her proclamation does not endear her to me. But given that I'm not in control of tonight's schedule—yet another thing that pisses me off—I nod, and the room empties.

Holly stalks out from behind the screen and begins stripping and yelling at the same time. I follow her, but at a slight distance.

"If you ever refer to me as *Mrs. Creighton Karas* in that tone again, I'll be writing a song about a nutless wonder to commemorate ripping your balls off."

I hold out both hands, but one drops slightly in an instinctive gesture to protect my testicles. She throws her button-down shirt on a chair and peels off her jeans.

I'm too caught up in staring at her perfect ass to formulate an intelligent response. Sometimes being a man has its disadvantages, but I refuse to think now is one of those times. It turns out I don't need to say anything, because Holly has plenty to say.

"I thought maybe, just maybe, after I explained things to you last night, you'd get it. But you don't. You just *don't*. I've already walked out on you once, and if you'd like *not* to be left behind when I drive off in that fancy new bus you had delivered today, we need to get some things straight."

My eyes narrow, and my tone is dangerous. "Do continue. I'd love to know what things we need to get straight."

Her eyes flash, equally dangerous. "The only way this

is ever going to work is if you understand that I consider my career to be just as important as yours. I might not pull down billions, but this—" her arm swings out wide, "is my dream. I've given up *everything* to have this chance, and I'm not going to waste it."

She's talking like I didn't listen to a single word she said last night in our hotel room.

"Do you think I'd be sitting in this shithole of a room, working on my phone, if I didn't consider what you want important? I've rarely so much as walked across the street to go out of my way for a woman I've been with. They've all been carefully selected to fit into my life and be convenient, but not you."

I pause, gripping her chin and lifting it so I can stare directly into her eyes. "*You* are decidedly inconvenient. And yet, here I am. Because I want you however I can get you, and I think I've made that pretty fucking clear."

The muscles of her jaw work against my fingers, and she whispers, "I don't want to be treated like an afterthought."

"You're not an afterthought. Jesus Christ, Holly. When you look at me like that, you're my only fucking thought."

I release her chin and she melts into me, her tense look fading away. I lean in to kiss her, but that feisty attitude of hers flares up again.

"So you'll calm down when it comes to me getting changed in my own freaking dressing room?"

That feistiness brings my club-wielding caveman alter ego back to life. "Not even a little bit. You're my wife; therefore the only person who is going to see that gorgeous ass or those luscious tits is me." I think for a second. "Or a licensed medical professional."

"My stylists are going to see me in my underwear. That's non-negotiable."

I tilt my head and speak directly into her ear. "As long as your stylists all either have pussies or are male and flaming homosexuals, I can live with that. Otherwise, you're going to have a problem." I nip her earlobe with my teeth. "And that problem's going to be an ass so red you won't sit for a week."

I wait for her to explode into another tirade, but she just whispers, "If you meant that to be a warning, you missed the mark."

My cock jumps in my pants and I open my mouth to respond, but Holly just smiles a sassy little sex-kitten smile and slips out of my arms.

"I'm not done with you, woman." I follow her across the room.

She grabs a dress off a hanger, unzips the back, and steps in. "Good to know, but I'm on a timeline. I don't have time to stop and screw right now."

Have I mentioned how much I love her unfiltered thoughts? If not, that's an oversight on my part.

She presents me with her back. "Can you get the zipper?"

"No."

I cross to the door and lock it.

"Take the dress off."

CHAPTER
ELEVEN

Creighton

Holly spins around, holding the dress against her chest. "Are you crazy? I have to get ready."

"We've still got the rest of our ten minutes. What kind of man would I be if I let that go to waste?"

She doesn't move as I close the distance between us. "Take the dress off, Holly."

I love watching the goose bumps rise on her arms and the shiver that grips her. *Oh yes, she's my dirty girl.*

She opens her mouth to speak.

"The only word I want to hear coming out of that beautiful mouth is yes."

The dress falls forward as Holly releases her hold on it. I help her step out of it and lay it over the back of a chair. Then I scan the room with new eyes and settle on the vanity.

"I may not be able to mess up your hair or makeup, but I'm going to stare into those gorgeous eyes while I'm pounding into you."

Holly's chest heaves with deep breaths as she steps toward the vanity. She pauses, as if waiting for my instructions.

Fucking. Perfect.

"Hands on the table."

She complies, and her big brown eyes stare back at me in the reflection of the mirror.

"Spread your legs."

One bare foot slides a few inches to the right.

"More."

Her other foot slides a few inches to the left. I step between her legs, pressing a hand to her lower back, and push her feet apart.

She's still wearing a tiny thong, and I don't hesitate to give the waistband a tug to snap it. Through every movement, we never break eye contact. I flick open the button of my jeans and unzip, freeing my cock. I'm already rock hard and dying to be inside her.

I fist my dick and say, "Be quiet, or I'll have to gag you. Do you understand?" I don't carry a gag in my pocket, but I'm sure I could find an adequate substitute.

"I can be quiet," she whispers.

"You sure?"

"Yes. Please. I need you."

The grin that stretches across my face reflects back at me as I stare into her eyes. "You better hold on, baby, and be quiet. Because I'm going to do everything I can to make you scream my name."

I fit myself to her entrance and drive into her soaked pussy. Our groans echo in the small room before we both stifle them. Gripping her with both hands, I pull out and thrust again and again into the tightest, sweetest cunt I've ever had the pleasure to fuck.

And it's all mine. *Mine.* I don't even realize I've said the word aloud until I see Holly's eyes flash in the mirror and she mouths the word *yours.*

Wanting her mindless with pleasure, I vary my strokes. As I find her clit with my fingers, it doesn't take much for me to push her over the edge into a silent orgasm. I follow, just as silently, and hate that I'm not able to yell her name as I empty myself inside her.

She's slumped on the vanity when I pull out, and I use her wrecked thong to catch my cum as it slips out of her. I meet her eyes again in the mirror. They're bright and fevered, and I want to turn her around and fuck her again, but she says, "I've never wanted to skip a meet and greet before. Never. But right now . . . damn it. I can't."

"It's okay. You have more underwear?" She shakes her head, and I swear. "And you think you're going out there in front of all those people with nothing on under that dress? No fucking way. Not a goddamn chance."

Her laugh is low and husky, and my dick perks up again at the sound. "You know I'm fucking with you, right? I have Spanx that go on under it. Not as sexy, but definitely required."

I open my mouth to say something else, but a knock

followed by the sound of the door handle jiggling stalls my words. Tossing her panties into the trash, I go answer it while she retrieves her Spanx.

The woman from earlier looks put out that the door is locked. She looks even more put out when I won't let her in.

"Give us another minute."

She bristles. "She's going to be late if she doesn't hurry."

"Two fucking minutes. I'm not asking."

"Fine. But hurry."

I shut the door in her face, resisting the urge to slam it. I don't like that woman. At all. I have to remind myself that she's just doing her job, and her job is to help Holly. For that, I won't do whatever I would need to in order to get her ass fired.

I turn and once again, Holly has her back to me, waiting for assistance with the zipper. I slide it up, my eyes drinking in the smooth skin that was under my palms only minutes ago. She does a sexy little shimmy and straightens the dress before reaching for her boots. She slides her feet in one at a time and turns to me, and her bright pink lips curve into a shy smile.

The shyness is ironic considering what we just did.

"How do I look?"

I take her in from head to toe. Dark waves that curl to midway down her back. Snapping brown eyes with thick black lashes. The slick pink lips I'd like wrapped around my cock. A tiny silver excuse for a dress barely covering curves that could stop traffic. Toned legs I want my face between. Turquoise cowboy boots with black-and-silver angel wings embroidered on them that I'd probably let walk all over me.

Christ, this woman is like none other; she's a complete contradiction. An innocent sex kitten. A tentative temptress. My every fantasy wrapped up in a package that's more dangerous to handle than dynamite.

"You look fucking beautiful. If I didn't give a shit about your career, I'd kidnap you and drag you off to some harem in the desert where men can still own women like property." I shake my head. "You need to get out of this room before I can't let you leave."

Her eyes, still bright from her orgasm, blink twice before she swallows and crosses to the door.

I follow her out into the hallway, and the dingy gray walls are blocked by three security guys the size of the Alps. They eye me suspiciously, and I return the favor. I don't like the idea of people who aren't on my payroll protecting her. That needs to be remedied. Holly's too precious to put at risk.

As it turns out, I have more reason to be concerned because they aren't there to protect her; they're forming a wall around Boone Thrasher.

Two women are being dragged down the hallway screaming, "Boone! We love you!"

He's holding a red lacy bra in one hand and a black thong in the other. He tosses both to one of the security guys. The man looks less than thrilled to be handling what was presumably covering some women's tits and ass until just recently.

"Do . . . whatever you do with this shit," he grunts.

His smirk turns into a megawatt grin when he notices Holly.

"Hey, sugar. You ready to kick some ass tonight? Glad to see you didn't pull a John Denver on your way here, because I know you fucking flew." He steps toward her and pulls her into a hug.

Even knowing he's in a relationship with his own country starlet, I'm hard-pressed not to break his god-damn arms. I wasn't fucking around when I said I'd like to take her away and keep her to myself.

His security team eyes me and the pass hanging around my neck carefully when I make a move toward her. Holly retreats from Thrasher's hold and tucks a long lock of hair behind her ear.

Thrasher finally notices me and smirks. My expression must be a fuck of a lot more dangerously possessive than I realized, because he says, "Didn't mean to steal your new bride, man. Thanks for not punching me in the throat; I need my vocal cords for my set."

He offers his hand and I shake it, careful not to crush it in my grip. He probably needs those fingers to play a fucking banjo.

"Thrasher."

"Karas. You taking good care of this girl here?"

Holly interjects. "Did you see my new bus? I think it might be nicer than yours."

Thrasher's head bobs a few times. "Yeah. Fucking puts us all to shame. But no matter. I like seeing you spend money on this girl. She deserves it. Good woman." His expression sharpens. "Just be sure you're clear on the fact that she ain't the kind of girl you can buy."

Holly lays a hand on my arm, eyelashes batting in my direction, and her drawl sounds thicker than ever. "Creighton would never think I'm the kind of girl he can buy. He values his equipment too much to risk it." She tilts her head, her expression turning mischievous. "Although he probably has it insured. The man *is* proud of what he's packing below the belt."

Thrasher's security detail guffaws, and I swear Thrasher glances down at my dick. I just shake my head at Holly's sassiness once again making an appearance. Being teased isn't something I'm used to, but with her, I don't mind it.

Thrasher gives me a chin jerk. "That ain't a half-bad idea. My dick is worth its weight in gold, no doubt. A whole hell of a lot of gold."

And now I know the hick has a big dick.

The woman from Holly's dressing room earlier interrupts. "Excuse me, Boone, but we need to get Holly to the meet and greet. Her fans are waiting."

"Can't keep your fans waiting. Go get 'em, girl. I'll see you onstage for 'That Girl' later."

"You sure will."

Thrasher's off through the hallways, his security detail leading the way and following closely behind.

"Where's your security?" I ask Holly as we follow the woman.

"I don't really have dedicated people. One of Boone's guys will usually show up in the meet-and-greet room and keep tabs just in case the venue security doesn't show. If I have to walk through a crowd, one of his guys will cover me, or venue security will help there too if Boone's people can't be spared."

My teeth grind together. "That's changing tomorrow. You'll have someone following you everywhere at a venue, and in public, if I'm not with you."

"That's not really necessary."

We pause outside what I presume is the meet-and-greet room, and I tilt her face up to mine. "It's absolutely necessary. And not just because of your career, but because of me. You could be a target, and I'm not going to let anything happen to you." I'm not entirely certain, but I think it's shock I see flash across her face.

"Holly. Let's go," the woman calls from inside the room. She's really starting to piss me off.

"We'll talk about it after the show," is Holly's only response before she ducks inside the door.

I follow her inside and prepare to spend the next hour holding up a corner while almost a hundred fans wait their turn to meet Holly and get a quick picture and autograph. I'm surprised by who I see in line. It's not just the bouncing—and some crying—teenage girls and the soccer moms. It's also young guys looking to press up against her, and older men who hug her too tightly. I want to feed the women some Xanax and rip the hands and dicks off the men.

After about fifteen minutes, a guy wearing black skinny jeans that show way too much of his package, black cowboy boots, and a black pearl-snap shirt embroidered with white horses, stops directly in front of me and holds out a bottle of Budweiser.

"You look like you could use a beer."

When I accept the bottle with thanks and shake his outstretched hand, he says, "I'm Chance, Holly's manager."

"Creighton Karas."

"I know," he says, his accent thick and clearly of the good-ole-boy variety. "You're Holly's new husband. For a minute, anyway."

My eyes narrow on his smug hazel ones. "Is that your guess, or is that the word on the street?"

He tips his own beer back, and I'm mildly surprised to see he's drinking while he's on the job. I guess the music industry is a little different from corporate America.

"Both," he replies. "I was glad to see the back of JC. He wasn't doing nothing for her, and she was just getting dragged into his drama further and further."

I sense the direction this conversation is taking, and I'm not sure I want to go there, but what the hell. I tip back my beer and take a swig.

"And me?"

"Holding out judgment until I see if you last more than one day on tour. This ain't your billionaire-boys'-club lifestyle. This shit is hard work, nonstop, and it ain't got nothing to do with you."

Considering I've been trailing along like a lap dog today after Holly, I think I'm starting to understand what he means. The woman works her ass off and never seems to take a break. No wonder she ducked out of the penthouse at the first down moment she had.

Most women in my acquaintance would have spent their time checking out the designer wardrobe I ordered, but not Holly. And considering how she spent her morning, scribbling away in her notebook, it doesn't take a genius to figure out that she didn't think twice about doing whatever she had to in order to work on her songs—including finding the nearest guitar. I wonder how many she's written since the wedding, and what's more, if she'll ever play any of them for me.

I decide not to respond to Chance's question, but instead ask, "When does her next album come out?"

He looks rather surprised that I'm asking. "It's due out early spring. She's got a break after the tour and then studio time back in Nashville. We've got a songwriter meeting up with us tomorrow to help hammer things out now that she's got more songs due, from what I hear. She didn't do too well writing when we were on the road before. She mostly stared off into space a lot and chewed on the end of her pen."

"She's been writing nonstop all day, and she wrote when she was in New York as well, so I'm assuming she's got the situation handled."

His eyebrows shoot up. "No shit? Then maybe you are good for something, Bill."

Bill? What the fuck?

Chance reads my confusion as he sucks back another drink. "Billionaire. Bill. I do nicknames. That's yours."

I open my mouth to rip him a new asshole, when I hear Holly make a sound of distress. My attention zeroes in on her, and I'm across the room before I know what the fuck I'm doing.

There's a guy, probably around twenty-five, bending

her back over his arm, his mouth crushed against hers.

Not. Fucking. Happening.

I rip the guy away from her, and Holly stumbles back and steadies herself. My fist is already flying, catching the guy in the face with a right hook and then an uppercut to the gut. He drops to the floor and security is crowding around us. I don't register the flashes coming from all around me.

Where the fuck was security sixty seconds ago?

I turn, finding Holly behind a mountain of muscle. *About fucking time.* He steps aside, and I take in her pale features and smeared lipstick.

I spin back around, intent on going after the guy again, but the same mountain of muscle is already dragging him from the room. Lucky prick. Otherwise he'd be spending the night in the hospital.

Chance starts clearing the room, but Holly speaks up. "No. It's fine. I'm fine. I can finish the meet and greet. They've been waiting."

I step closer and frame her face with my hands, my thumbs wiping away the smears of red on her lips and cheek. "You don't need to do that."

"They're my fans. They're the reason I have a career, and the only reason I'll continue to have a career. It's no big deal. It's not like it's the first time some guy has decided he wanted a kiss."

My thoughts turn volcanic. "That security I mentioned? You will have two people on you at all times when you're in a venue. That shit isn't happening again."

"It's not necessary," she argues.

I lean in and murmur, "It's absolutely necessary. And if you don't want me to kiss the fuck out of you right now to erase that asshole's taste from your lips, you better say so pretty damn quick."

"But the fans—"

"Let them watch. You're mine. I don't care who sees."

Her mouth drops open into a small O, but she doesn't voice a protest.

I take that as my green light and lower my lips to hers, but I don't crush them to her like that motherfucker did. I kiss her softly. Gently. Softer and more gently than I've ever kissed her before. And in that moment, I wonder why I haven't taken the time to savor her.

Her lips soften, her mouth opens, and my tongue slips inside, teasing and stroking hers. I release her slowly. Her closed eyelids flutter open, her brown eyes soft and warm.

She swallows as I pull away. "Thank you. I didn't realize I needed that."

"I didn't realize I needed that so much either."

I lower my hands from her face and step back. "I'll let you get back to your fans then."

The bossy woman from earlier steps up with an open bottle of water, a mirror, and lipstick. "Take a drink, then we'll get you fixed up. But we need to pick up the pace. We're running out of time."

Holly's eyes stay on mine as she accepts the water and takes a reluctant sip. I step away and return to my corner.

Chance has already arranged for someone to clean up the shattered remains of the beer bottle I dropped when I lunged at the prick kissing Holly. He's holding out another beer when I return to the corner. As I grab it and take a long pull, he pats me on the shoulder.

"You just might do, Bill. You just might do."

CHAPTER TWELVE

Holly

The heat of the lights.

The rhythmic beat of the bass guitar and the drums.

The sound of the crowd singing along to the lyrics of my first single.

I blink back tears as I hold the microphone out and empty my lungs on the final note. The lights go dark, and for a second the venue is silent before screams erupt. I close my eyes and bite my lip, laughing silently to myself.

This.

This is what it's all about. This feeling makes it all worth it. This feeling is part of the reason why I walked into a hotel room and married a perfect stranger only hours later. Because I can't imagine never feeling like this again.

I let my head fall back and stare up at the blackness before the roadies start rushing around the stage and clearing my stuff out. I take a deep breath, and my mind instantly goes to the man waiting offstage.

I felt his eyes on me the entire time. Before tonight, I might have worried that Creighton would spend the entire set watching and judging me, but his actions in the meet-and-greet room tilted everything off its axis. Not just the fact that he went after the drunk punk who decided he wanted a kiss, but Creighton's own kiss after that. I expected the caveman or the possessive asshole, but what I got was something altogether different.

He's already changing, and I still haven't figured out the first Creighton I met. All day, he's been nothing like I imagined he would be. He hasn't once tried to make today about him or his business. He's been, for the most part, at my side and supportively following me around.

Don't expect it to last, Holly. Right now this relationship is a novelty to him. It'll wear off soon enough.

He's a thirty-three-year-old billionaire; how could he possibly be content to follow me around? He has an empire to run, and I don't know how he can possibly run it from a tour bus. There's no way he would have made it through the long haul before our Christmas break. Part of me wished this second leg of the tour was longer so I could let it test him.

And then the cynic in me—or maybe it's the realist—also chimes in with much more pertinent and troubling questions.

What if he didn't like the show? What if the best part of

me isn't good enough for him? Then what do I have to offer?

Self-doubt eats away the after-show high I'm riding, because what else do I have to offer? My pretty face and my apparently magic pussy? Is my only use in being seen—with my legs spread—and not heard?

The questions echo on repeat, kicking my heart rate up faster, until all I can hear is the rush of blood in my ears. At least that drowns out the sound of my mama's voice telling me I'll never be anything more than a girl from the trailer park, no matter how many stages I sing on.

A roadie accidentally clips me on the shoulder, and I stumble back into reality.

"Sorry!"

"It's fine. I'm in the way."

I regain my balance and walk toward the edge of the stage, trying to reinforce the crumbling walls of my confidence and self-respect.

Thousands of fans were screaming my name. Singing along. Begging for more. What is one man's opinion compared to that? But he's not just any man. He's my husband.

Sweet baby Jesus. Why did I do this? I thought I could marry him and be unaffected, but already I'm letting the thought of his disapproval drive what little hard-won self-assurance I have into the ground.

With JC, I never had to worry about that. But I was the girl who chose to jump from a fake, mostly-gay boyfriend to a very real, very out-of-my-league husband.

I search the edge of the stage and see Creighton leaning against a speaker. Every woman in the vicinity has her gaze riveted on him, and I don't blame them. His arms are crossed, and his golden tan contrasts with the rolled-up cuffs of his white dress shirt. Dark hair is sprinkled across his defined muscles. Even in jeans, which I'm still shocked he owns, he manages to look every inch the ridiculously rich playboy.

His eyes drill into me as I dodge roadies, cords, speakers, and instruments, telling myself that I have no reason to feel inferior to this man, but that doesn't mean I believe it. I'm still in the *fake-it-'til-you-make-it* stage of the process.

I desperately want to know what he thought of my performance. The question is bubbling up inside me. *I will not ask.* I have to grind my teeth to hold it in. In my world, that's just inviting criticism. Despite my vow, the question comes tumbling out as soon as I'm standing before him.

My smile I wear for the cameras when I really want to run away is in place. "So, what did you think?"

He uncrosses his arms and pushes off the speaker. My heart hammers in my chest as he opens his mouth and then closes it again without speaking. He takes one step toward me, his frown in place.

I wrap my arms around my body, prepared to ward off a verbal blow.

"I watched you last night."

Shock zings through me at his statement. "In San Antonio? I thought you were just waiting outside to drag me home by my runaway-wife hair."

"No. I watched the whole damn thing, and you're insane if you think you shouldn't be headlining these shows."

I think my heart stutters to a stop . . . and then restarts with heavy, tripping beats.

"What?" I whisper.

"You're too good to be an opening act. I don't know shit about the music industry, and I didn't think I'd like country music, but I like your music. You've got this voice that grabs a man by the throat and won't let go until the last note fades."

Speechless, I swallow. Creighton reaches out to wrap his hand around my upper arm and steady me.

I'm still recovering from his confession when he asks, "Where to now?"

"Um, backstage for a little bit, and then they'll come get me for 'That Girl.'"

His hand slides down my arm to lace his fingers with mine. I let him lead me out back into the hallway toward my dressing room. We hear chants and screaming from Boone's room as we pass.

People try to talk to me, but I don't hear them. I just follow Creighton, staring at the white dress shirt stretching across his shoulders as his words play on repeat in my head.

"I like your music . . . You've got this voice that grabs a man by the throat and won't let go until the last note fades . . ."

You'd think his compliments would banish the insecurity that's settled inside me, but instead they unleash a way bigger problem.

I think I could fall for my husband.

CHAPTER
THIRTEEN

Holly

"Don't stop. *Please. Don't stop."* My throaty moan is porn-star worthy.

Creighton's growl vibrates against my clit, and the fingers of one hand grip my hip tighter.

Part of me hopes I'll have bruises to prove he touched me there. I need some reminder that his amazing Grade-A, blue-ribbon-winning skills are real. Seriously. He deserves an honorary degree from some fancy-pants university for his talents in this area.

I buck my pelvis against his mouth, desperate to get more, and eager to find the edge so I can sail off into an orgasm. I earn a sharp slap to my thigh.

"Hold still, or I won't let you come."

"Oh God, please," I moan.

He lifts his head away, his fingers still buried inside me, and I whimper at the loss of stimulation. "You'll take what I give you, when I give it to you."

"I'm already begging. What more do you want from me? Just let me come!"

My eyes flick open as a deep chuckle fills the expanse of my brand-new tour bus. Right now, I couldn't care less how shiny, fancy, new, and overwhelming it is. I just want to come.

"Bossy thing. Guess it works out that I can't get enough of this sweet little cunt of yours."

I know I should climb up on a soapbox and tell him I don't like that word. The c-word. But my brain has no control over the flood of wetness that hits my center when he says it.

He doesn't miss it. The two fingers buried in my pussy curl forward, stroking my G-spot.

"Fuck, baby, you're so wet."

"Say it again."

"You're so—"

"No. What you said before." I'm babbling now, and I don't care. I just want more of his dirty words and his devastating tongue.

"That I can't get enough of this sweet little cunt?"

My inner muscles clench, and he groans. I wish I had the coordination to reach down and stroke his cock, but I'm slumped back on the black leather sofa, and he's down on his knees before me.

The thought that I've somehow brought this man to his knees is enough to shove me to the edge of orgasm.

"I'm going to come."

Creighton lifts his head again. "No, you're not. Because I'm not done eating your pussy yet."

"But—"

"You'll wait until I give you permission."

Creighton lowers his mouth to my pussy and laps at the juices before flicking, nipping, and teasing my clit. I dig my nails into the new leather, not caring what marks I may leave, because suddenly I don't want to disappoint him by coming before he allows me. The pleasure rises harder and faster, and my control begins to disintegrate.

I open my mouth to beg yet again, but Creighton's words come first, directly against my clit.

"Come for me. Now. Hard."

I slam my eyes shut as the tension inside me bursts, surging within me and spreading out through every nerve ending. I lose complete control, bucking against him and burying my hands in his hair as I scream his name.

I ride the sensations, and his continued teasing, until I can't handle any more. I tug his head up and melt into the couch. Holy. Shit. I'd say the man's tongue should be bronzed, but that would be a waste.

I'm still lazily floating in the post-orgasmic haze, enjoying Creighton's hand smoothing up and down my inner thigh and the press of lips on my hipbone, when someone knocks on the door to the bus.

"Tell them to go away," I whine.

At any other moment, I might care that I sound like a little brat, but right now, I really, really don't. All I want is to savor this feeling for a few more minutes, and then give my own knees a workout while I return the favor.

Creighton complies with my request, and his deep voice punctures the bus's silence. "Go the fuck away!"

Points for style to Creighton.

The knock comes again.

"Ugh. Really?"

I open my eyes and look toward the clock. Something about nine a.m. is nagging at my brain. We already hit a seven a.m. radio spot, and this little interlude was my reward for actually rolling out of bed on time. Well, that's what I'm calling it anyway.

Creighton rises, eyeing my body, which is naked from the waist down. "As much as I hate to say it, you need to put some more clothes on."

I let out a grumbling groan that is the opposite of sexy. Luckily, Creighton just smiles and adds, "I'll get the door and distract whoever it is."

As I peel myself off the couch and stumble toward the back bedroom of the bus, I have a sneaking suspicion that this is what teamwork feels like. And isn't that what a marriage is supposed to be? Teamwork?

This one-week-old marriage of impulse is starting to feel more real every day, and I'm not certain how I feel about that. It was supposed to be simple. Uncomplicated. An easy way for me to dodge the JC-fake-fiancée situation and try to take some control over my own career—and indulge in a lot more orgasms like the one I just had. But it's quickly morphing into something else entirely.

Do I want it to be something else? Am I really prepared to make this a real marriage? Is Creighton?

I press my thumb and forefinger into my temples, which are starting to ache. I need time to sit and consider this change in our regularly scheduled program so I can decide how to react—but it's not like I've got many spare minutes to sit and ponder while on tour. I can't help but wonder if it's just the fact that Creighton is out of his element that's causing things to change.

What happens after the tour? The ache in my head ratchets up to a throb. *Great. Don't have time for a headache.*

Male voices come from the living area of the bus, and I hurriedly slip on a pair of yoga pants and glance in the mirror. My hair and my expression clearly communicate *just been fucked*—which isn't really fair. Yes, I just had an orgasm, but things were just starting to get good when we were interrupted.

Heading back out to the living area of the bus, still bowled over by the granite countertops, leather couches, and dark cherrywood interior that is altogether fancier than any bus I've ever been on before, I remember why nine a.m. was nagging at me.

Because I have an appointment scheduled. With a songwriter. Except no one bothered to tell me it was Vale Garcia.

Fudge sticks.

I plaster on a congenial smile. "Look what the cat dragged in," I drawl.

Vale's grin is knowing, and I fight the urge to grit my teeth.

"Didn't mean to interrupt," he says.

Creighton looks from Vale to me. "I take it you two have worked together before?"

Vale stares at me as he answers Creighton. "Holly and I worked *very* closely together right after she won *Country Dreams*. Isn't that right, Hols?"

He couldn't be any more obvious than if he scrawled the words *I did everything but bang your wife* in fat black Sharpie on a yellow neon piece of poster board and waved it around over his head. Except to a casual observer, Vale's smug smile probably did say *I banged your wife*—which isn't true.

I respond with what I hope is ego-deflating nonchalance. "The last year has been such a whirlwind, I can barely remember what I was doing a few minutes ago." I slide in closer to Creighton and glance up at him. "Well, that's not entirely true. Some things I remember *very* vividly."

Smiling back at Vale, I wonder if my expression looks half as smug as I think it does. "I apologize; I'm being so rude. Vale, this is my husband, Creighton Karas. Creighton, this is Vale Garcia."

Vale reaches out, and he and Creighton shake hands, clearly taking each other's measure.

"I guessed," Vale says, dropping Creighton's hand after a moment. His eyes cut back to me. "Still surprised you decided to settle down with a one-night stand. Thought you were against those?"

Creighton's shoulders stiffen. "I'd watch what you say right about now, Mr. Garcia. You're speaking about my wife." His tone communicates barely leashed anger.

"I don't mean anything by it. Just jealous, I guess. I'm

big enough to admit that I wish I could've been the one to catch her."

I clear my throat. "All right then. Moving on. Vale, while don't you settle in, and I'll grab my notes."

The man might be an asshole who stomped out of my hotel room when I wouldn't let him complete his slide into home base—only to find his way into another woman's room only a few hours later—but he's also a damn good songwriter.

Creighton's arm tenses under my palm, and I'm pretty clear on the fact that he doesn't want Vale anywhere near me, especially not alone.

I drag Creighton toward the bedroom with me. Well, drag is a bit of an overstatement. I'm under no illusions that he's following my tugging grip for any reason other than he wants to.

Once I pull him into the room and shut the door, I blurt, "I didn't sleep with him. It was a close thing, which I'm sure you picked up on, but what I told you before was true. It had been a long time for me before you. Anyway, I want you to know that there's absolutely no reason to get weird about Vale."

Creighton's eyes are practically burning holes in me. "This isn't me getting weird, Holly. This is me getting fucking jealous." He jams a hand into his thick brown hair. "And I don't fucking like it. I hate knowing that he's touched you."

I'm silent, because I honestly have no idea how to respond. But then again, I'm also aware that Vale is waiting. He's about to wait a little longer.

I grab a fistful of Creighton's T-shirt and yank him toward me. "Then kiss me. Mark me. Let him know that I'm absolutely and completely out of his reach because I belong to you."

Where those words—hell, those thoughts—came from, I have no idea. I've rebelled against the very idea of being Creighton's possession since the day we said "I do," but this is something totally different. This is something I'm desperate for. I'm not willing to put a label on it yet, and it's nothing I've ever wanted in my life. At least, not that I would admit to before.

Creighton studies me, and I'm not sure what he concludes, but he doesn't hesitate to wrap his arm under my ass and haul me up against him. His mouth lands on mine with an almost crazed intensity. It's all lips and teeth and tongue as we devour each other.

I throw one arm around his neck and scrape the nails of my other hand along the back of his neck and up into his hair. The kiss lasts only a minute—maybe two—but when he lowers me to the floor, my legs are shaking and my heart is hammering so hard, I feel like it could break a rib.

That just-been-fucked look? I don't need to look in the mirror to know I'm now sporting it in spades. My panties are soaked, and there's nothing I want more in this moment than to beg him to bend me over the bed and bang the hell out of me.

"You're so goddamn beautiful." He leans in. "And you're mine. Don't forget it, and don't you let him fucking forget it."

My nod is jerky, and Creighton turns, yanks open the door, and stalks out of the room. I ease the door shut again with trembling fingers and quickly strip out of my yoga pants, change my underwear, and jam my legs into a pair of jeans.

I take a deep, relaxing breath, attempting to slow my heart rate back down to a level that doesn't feel like it's about to explode. When I exit the bedroom, notebook in hand, Creighton is lingering at the front of the bus and Vale is settled into a chair, notebook propped up on the arm and his guitar in his lap.

Creighton's eyes snap to me, and my feet take me directly in front of him without any conscious thought on my part. He brushes my hair away from my face and cups my jaw. "I need to go take care of something. I'll be back in a few hours."

His explanation is vague and my curiosity is piqued. What could Creighton possibly need to do in Dallas that would take a few hours? But I don't question him.

I'm learning to trust, I tell myself. *After all, isn't that what he's doing by leaving me alone with Vale?*

"Okay. Want to plan to meet up at noon for lunch? I've got a radio thing from two to three, and then I'm free until I have to get ready for the meet and greet."

"That works for me," Creighton says.

I close the distance between us and lean up on my tiptoes to press a kiss to his lips. "One more for the road," I whisper, feeling very wife-like.

I'm still absorbing that thought when he steps away and again brushes a lock of hair behind my ear, leaving my own taste on my lips. I like knowing I've marked him too.

"One will never be enough," he replies before his lips skim across mine once more. He turns and heads for the door.

I'm still standing there like a love-struck fool when he steps off the bus.

I lower my guitar with the last chord of "Lost on Fifth Avenue" hanging in the air between Vale and me. He's silent for long moments, and my heart rate kicks up, waiting for his opinion. I might think it's awesome, but he's the one with a couple of Grammys on his shelf, and all I have is instinct.

Finally, Vale speaks. "You're going to kill it with that song. Absolutely kill it. You've come a hell of a long way since the last project we worked on, if all your stuff is like this now."

My heart thuds even harder. "You think it's . . . good?"

"Holly, this song is the shit. I've been doing this long enough to know what's good and what's really fucking good, and you've just written a chart-topper, girl. I take it you wrote this one recently."

He raises an eyebrow. Given the lyrics, it's clear that I wrote it after I met Creighton in New York. The song is all about feeling small in the big city, and realizing that as long as you have at least one thing anchoring you, you can't get too lost.

When I originally started writing it, the anchor I was

talking about was my music . . . but listening to it now, I know that the anchor is not a thing, but a person. This man that I'm way too attached to.

I remember that Vale asked a question. "Yes, I wrote it recently. I've got two more, if you don't think we need to rework this one."

He shakes his head. "Nah, I don't want to fuck with this one. Besides, if we start messing with it, then I'll have to take credit for part of it, and this one is really all you, babe."

His endearment hangs in the air, just like the earlier chords did.

"I probably shouldn't call you that, huh? The billionaire will come rip my balls off and feed them to me."

A chuckle slips from my lips. "He's a little territorial."

"With good reason. I'm just glad the man knows he's got his hands on someone he needs to treasure. I didn't get that before it was too late. You're a special woman, Holly Wix, and whatever emotions he's pulled from you, they're going to shine bright in your songs. Have you played them for him?"

I blink a few times. "Played them for him? Um, no. No, I haven't."

I think about the next song I'm going to play for Vale, and my stomach rolls. I bare my soul in these lyrics, and to an average fan, it's not a big thing. But to someone who actually knows me? I might have written the thing in my own blood because that's my heart written right on the lined notebook paper. My hopes, but mostly my fears.

"You realize he's going to hear them eventually, right?

That's kind of what you do." Vale has his head tilted and he's speaking slowly, like I'm an idiot.

"I know, but . . . I hadn't thought that far ahead."

His eyebrows go up. "Didn't expect the marriage to last long enough for the record to come out first?"

My glare is automatic, but the answer is probably written on my face anyway. I still, even now, have a hard time seeing how this is going to work, and long-term isn't a concept I've let myself get comfortable with. My life has been so focused on just making it from one day to the next that I haven't spent much time thinking about it.

"How about we move on to the next one? We've got," I glance at the clock on the wall, "a couple more hours, so we should use them wisely. After all, I've got five more songs to deliver for this big-box exclusive."

"The label is going to shift the entire record around after you turn this bad boy in. I wouldn't be surprised if it's the first single."

His words fill my chest with warmth, and I pick up my guitar and flip a page in my notebook. The rest of these are going to bare my soul just as much, so I might as well get through them and make them as good as they can possibly be. This is more than my career, this is my passion, and I'm blessed to have this chance—and lucky to have Vale's time.

"You ready to hear the next one?"

"Lay it on me, girl."

I begin to play, and the smile on his face grows. By the time I finish, he's rubbing his hands together.

"Okay, a few tweaks to the chorus, a rework of the

bridge, and I think this one is going to be fucking awesome too."

I reach for my pen. "Let's do it."

Vale packs up his guitar and leaves the bus at a quarter to twelve. We shake hands, and I feel like he's seeing me as a professional now, which is validation I didn't realize I wanted from him. I'm not just the naive girl who stepped off the stage of *Country Dreams*; I'm a rising talent in the world of country music, on both the songwriting and performing fronts.

With that confidence bolstering me, I tinker with the songs some more until the clock reads 12:20. Still no sign of Creighton.

My confidence in Creighton and not being an afterthought takes a blow, however. He's still gone, and he hasn't called. I'm interrupted from the slow slide into the pit of doubt by my buzzing cell phone—the one that arrived that arrived yesterday via express mail. Inside the box was a note from Tana.

Don't you dare let your focus slip from that tour to your husband's fine ass. This is your future, girl. Love ya, T.

Even long distance, she's still dispensing her brand of wisdom, and it was a good reminder.

My phone buzzes again, and I finally look down. I don't recognize the number, and normally I'd let it go to voice mail, but right now, I'll take any distraction I can get.

"Hello?"

"Will you accept a collect call from the Clay County Jail?" a computerized voice asks.

What the hell? I haven't gotten a call from jail in a long time. Not since the year before I moved in with Gran, and Mama was thrown out of a bar for fighting over her latest in a long string of men.

I should hang up, but my curiosity and need for avoidance spur me to respond, "Yes, I'll accept the charges."

The voice that comes next sucks me right back into the past.

"Hey, baby. Mama missed you."

CHAPTER
FOURTEEN

Creighton

After the fifteenth in-person interview is complete, I finally have two competent security professionals assigned to Holly. The security contractor didn't object to me doing the interviews, but he did object to me bringing in someone who wasn't on his team.

"We can't vouch for him, and if something goes down, we won't be taking responsibility for it."

"I can vouch for him," I say, looking over my shoulder at the brick shithouse who barred me from getting backstage in San Antonio.

His name was easy to get, and his background check showed he was a three-tour Army combat vet formerly of the First Infantry Division.

The man proved his character to me when he turned

down my money, but I never would have considered letting him near Holly without a clean background check and a personal interview. He was late coming in from San Antonio, and now I'm running late for lunch with Holly.

A check of my watch shows I'm running *really* fucking late. As in, if I make it back to the bus in ten minutes, I'll be just in time to tag along to the radio spot.

Glancing at my two new hires, I wave my hand toward the Escalade. "Load up. Your new job starts now."

When we arrive back at the bus, it's empty. Chaz, the driver, is smoking a cigarette and shooting the shit with the crew. According to him, Holly left only a few minutes earlier.

We pile back into the Escalade and head for the highway, which is closed. For a goddamn presidential visit.

"Fuck!" I slam my fist against the dash.

"Sorry to say it, boss, but we ain't gonna make it on time. This ain't my hood, so I don't know the back roads like I would if we were in SA."

Earlier, I handed off the keys to Marcus, aka the brick shithouse. Ironically, he wasn't trained in evasive driving maneuvers like the other guy I hired, but considering he dodged roadside bombs in a Humvee, I feel pretty comfortable with him behind the wheel. It would remain to be seen who would be driving Holly around when I wasn't with her.

I scrub a hand over my face.

"Yeah. I know. Shit. By the time traffic clears, she'll probably already be on her way to the venue." I glance from Marcus to the guy in the rear of the SUV. "Let's head back, and I'll introduce you to her crew first, and then Holly. She might balk, but regardless of what she says, you stick to the plan. You report to me, not her."

The man in the back nods wordlessly.

From the driver's seat, I get an altogether different response. "You gonna be up shit creek for being late, boss?"

I think about how I left things with Holly.

"Then kiss me. Mark me. Let him know that I'm absolutely and completely out of his reach because I belong to you."

I'm not sure I'll ever forget her words. They're etched on my brain and have reverberated ever since she spoke them.

When I started down this road, I couldn't have envisioned ending up in this position. And I'm not talking about the fact that I'm in an Escalade with two bodyguards driving down the side streets of Dallas. I'm talking about the fact that I'm caught up in this woman in a way that I've never been with another. It might have started out as purely physical, but I should have whiplash from how fast things have changed.

Leaving her alone with Vale went against all my possessive instincts, but I'm finding that I trust her, which is a new development for me. My last marriage, as short as it was, left me with a healthy distrust of women.

I met Shaw when I purchased a chain of luxury resorts off the auction block. It was founded by her grandfather and then run into the ground by her father before she could take control. She was ambitious, driven, and totally and completely pissed that her family legacy was circling the drain.

I tried to fire her, but she refused to leave, saying she'd work for free if I would just let her stay. I caved, and not only a little because her passion for the business was contagious. Shaw was an amazing leader of people. Charismatic, and also absolutely gorgeous.

I opted to take a personal role in the turnaround, and one thing led to another. We were a great team when it came to business, and more than compatible everywhere else. It made sense, or at least it did when Shaw pitched the idea to me like the skilled businesswoman she was. We were married within six months to the day I met her, and in a moment of generosity, I agreed in the prenup that she could keep the resorts if things didn't work out.

Three months after the wedding, I realized that the resorts were *all* she really wanted out of the deal. This was the first and only time I met someone who was a cagier negotiator than I was.

She was in love with someone else the entire time, and viewed me as the quickest and easiest way to reclaim her family legacy. The only thing that kept me from being crazy bitter about the way she coldly ended it was that righteous bitch, karma.

Shaw didn't end up with everything she wanted, because she lost the guy she truly loved. Apparently he wasn't the type to swallow the idea of his woman marrying another man. I couldn't blame the guy, and Shaw has since retreated into her hardnosed businesswoman persona, and the fun, playful side I caught glimpses of never emerged again, as far as I know.

Shortly after the divorce, I discovered that the problem with giving a woman a chain of resorts as a divorce settlement was the growing number of women eager to be the next ex-Mrs. Creighton Karas. The line of them grew long and creative, and I didn't trust a single one.

Marrying Holly was a great way to put a stop to the women desperate for my attention. I'm not proud that entered into my motivations, but I wasn't going to apologize for anything that got me to this point with this woman.

"Boss?" Marcus prompts, dragging me back to the here and now. "Shit creek?"

"Honestly, I'm not entirely sure. I'm still figuring her out."

A mix of a grunt and a chuckle comes from the other man in the car, Orrin Steel, a former SEAL who lost mobility in his left thumb and had to leave his team because of it. He opted to bow out of the Navy completely because he refused to ride a desk.

"You'll be trying to figure her out for the rest of your goddamn life. Women are a mystery best left unsolved," he adds.

Marcus erupts into laughter, and I'm still trying to decide if Holly's going to be pissed. The unfamiliar feeling of anxiety creeps in when I recall how she left only a two-word note before she walked out of my New York penthouse.

"You'd better drive faster," I say.

Holly climbs on the bus less than an hour after I return, but the initial feeling of relief I have at seeing her is wiped away when I take in the stooped set of her shoulders and pale face.

Flipping my laptop shut, I rise. "What's wrong?"

She skirts around me and sinks into a chair.

"Just a long day," she says, her tone defeated.

"Holly." I only say her name, but it carries a wealth of meaning. I know she's full of shit, and she knows I know she's full of shit.

"How do you feel about having a meet-the-parents day?"

Her question catches me off guard, especially because her shot at meeting my parents died the day my mother and father were killed in an attack on the African village where they moved us for their missionary work. It was a story I worked incredibly hard to keep out of the media to this day.

"Excuse me?" I ask.

Her eyes flick up at me from beneath dark lashes, and she says, "My mother may be coming to visit."

From what she's said about her mother, this new development shocks the shit out of me.

"Really?"

"Yeah, but only because I couldn't think fast enough to figure a way out of it."

"Well, that's honest."

"It was the call from jail that threw me off my game."

"Excuse me?" I repeat.

"If you weren't sure before that you married white

trash, you can rest assured that now you won't have any doubt. My mama was arrested for breaking and entering into my gran's house back home. Apparently the sheriff didn't have my number, so when I called the police station, they filled me in."

Holly's voice is weary, and she won't meet my eyes. "They wouldn't have even arrested her, but my mama broke up the sheriff's marriage before she left town by crowing about sleeping with him one night when she was drunk. His wife caught wind of it, and didn't believe him when he swore he hadn't. She left him, and he's never forgiven my mama. He also knew, like everyone in town, that Gran left me everything, including the house. So she had no right to be there at all."

"And that equates to her coming to visit, how?"

"I had to wire them money to bail her out of jail, and she has nowhere to go—that's why she was breaking into Gran's. When she asked to come here, I couldn't find the word *no* fast enough in my brain. Don't worry; she'll last a day or two, hook up with some roadie—"

Holly sucks in a deep breath and continues in a shakier tone. "And then I won't see her again until she runs out of the cash she'll steal from me and anyone else who isn't guarding their wallet. That's what happened when she tracked me down at the very beginning of the tour." Her voice breaks on the last word.

I cross the small living area of the bus, wrap her in my arms, and lift her into my lap as a few tears slip over her lids. I'm so shocked by the change from spitfire to hurt little girl that I have no idea how else to comfort her.

She leans against my shoulder for a beat before pulling back and climbing off my lap. She swipes at her eyes, smearing her mascara, and begins to pace.

"Damn it. I won't cry over her. I've cried over her too many times. She doesn't deserve any more of my tears. None."

"I agree. No one deserves your tears." *Not even me*, I add silently.

"And then there's you," she says.

"Me?" I ask.

Let's pause for one second and acknowledge the fact that this is a stupid fucking question for a guy to ask a woman at this particular juncture, but it's out of my mouth before I can call it back.

"Seriously? You stood me up. *Again*. And my mama, the gold digger, is coming to visit, and I'll have her yapping in my ear about how I'll never hold on to you unless I do something magical, like bleach my asshole or vajazzle my cooch, and even then, I'm probably not woman enough to keep a man like you."

Fuck. Holly's mother really did a number on her, and that woman will not find herself welcome here to continue the job. There's no way in hell I'll let her near Holly. I don't give a fuck who she is.

"I didn't expect it to take so long."

She crosses her arms, and I've done enough negotiating to know that her body language says she's closed off to any kind of reasonable interaction.

"What were you doing anyway?" she demands. When I open my mouth to respond, she holds up a hand, and I pause. "Never mind, you don't need to tell me. It's not like this is *that* kind of marriage anyway."

The acid in her tone puts my back up. I know she's pissed and emotional, but her taking swipes at what we're starting to build here pisses me off.

"And exactly what kind of marriage is this, Holly?" The question is a loaded one.

"We both know it's not going to last. I'm a passing fancy for you. And in case you're wondering, I'm not bleaching my asshole to keep you on the hook."

Her offbeat and slightly twisted sense of humor does the impossible; my pissed-off mood evaporates. I rise from the chair and move toward her, my predatory instincts taking over.

Pinning her to the fridge, I growl, "Not even if I ask nicely and promise to fuck that tight little asshole until you've come so many times your pleasure receptors are blown?"

She lifts her gaze to mine and mumbles, "I knew I shouldn't have said that."

I smooth the hair away from her face and lower my lips to her ear. "Don't ever be afraid to say anything to me."

When Holly doesn't reply, I pull away and stare down at her. "Holly. Look at me." I wait until she complies. "If you really believe what you said about this not lasting, then we have a serious problem."

Her teeth scrape her bottom lip, and she hesitates before asking, "Why?"

I infuse my words with steel, because I want there to be no confusion about the gravity of what I'm saying. "Because there's no way in hell I'm letting you go."

Her big brown eyes blink twice, and her mouth falls open. The spitfire who faded away for brief moments flares to life again.

"Who the hell are you, and what have you done with my *I'll be waiting in a hotel suite with a prenup and an engagement ring* husband?"

I cup her face with both hands, needing the contact. "Things change, Holly. And *everything* has changed for me because of you. If you haven't figured that out yet, then I'll just have to show you."

"I don't get you," she whispers.

I lower my forehead to hers and breathe her in. "That's where you're wrong. You've already got me."

She turns her head, breaking our contact. I drop my hands to my sides, and a shred of doubt filters into me, bringing a completely foreign feeling with it—uncertainty.

I consider crushing my lips to hers until her thoughts are filled with nothing and no one but me, but I also understand the value of backing off and letting her settle so I can return to claim victory another day. With the news of her mom's arrest and upcoming arrival, not to mention the unrelenting tour schedule, I suspect Holly is teetering on the edge of her breaking point right now, and the last thing I want to do is push her over.

This isn't about me. This is about her.

Deciding to change gears, I step away and nod toward the bus door.

"Want to meet your new security detail?" I ask.

"Security detail?"

"That's where I was. Doing personal interviews and reviewing background checks. I needed to make sure that I felt comfortable with them before I could bring them around you. If you have any issues with either of the guys, let me know, and we can replace them. But having said that, I think they're both solid choices." I meet her eyes. "I'm willing to trust them with your safety, and believe me when I say that isn't something I do lightly. At all."

Her posture relaxes for a fraction of a second, but tenses once more when she asks, "You think they can keep Mama away from me too?"

"Don't worry about her. I'll handle that myself."

CHAPTER
FIFTEEN

Holly

The energy from tonight's show is exactly what I need to shore up my inner reserves. The crowd was amazing, singing along and screaming. Maybe it's a sign that I'm a vain person, but there's really nothing like thousands of people chanting your name.

You'd think a girl from Gold Haven, Kentucky, who started off singing karaoke with the smell of fryer grease clinging to her hair and clothes wouldn't feel perfectly comfortable on a stage in front of ten thousand people, but I do. It's where I belong. Every time I get up there, it's with the absolute certainty that this is what I was born to do.

But just thinking about the past reminds me that Mama is coming to visit, and regardless of what Creighton says about taking care of her, she's going to find a way to dig her hooks into me. I just don't have thick enough armor when it comes to her. I want to call her back and tell her "hell no, I changed my mind," but I don't have any way to get in touch with her.

As I'm falling asleep on the bus, curled into Creighton's arms, the haze of orgasm steals my filter, and I tell him, "I wish I could turn back the clock and tell my mama to go somewhere else, *anywhere* else. I don't want her here. I don't want her messing with my life again. It never ends well."

Creighton squeezes me against his chest and presses a kiss to my hair. "Go to sleep. You've got another long day tomorrow in Biloxi."

The vibrations from the road and Creighton's steady, even breathing lull me into a dreamless sleep.

The next afternoon, I pull out my phone and check the time for the twentieth time in the last five minutes. Not because I'm worried I'm going to miss the Biloxi meet and greet, but because I keep expecting Mama to come barreling backstage and wreaking havoc like a raccoon sneaking into a house through a chimney.

Creighton shoots me a questioning look. "What are you doing? You're not going to be late, so calm the hell down."

I suck in a breath and release it slowly, trying to calm my nerves. "It's not that. It's Mama. I was hoping I'd get that out of the way early so I could get myself together for the show. I hate this feeling of being on edge."

Creighton's expression goes blank. "Shit. I forgot to tell you. She's taken care of."

I swear, everything in me slams to a halt—my lungs, my heart, the very blood in my veins. "What? What are you talking about?"

"I arranged for her to take a vacation. All expenses paid to Miami. I own a large portion of a resort there, and I figured it would give you the break you need. It was easy enough to get her to agree."

At his nonchalant announcement, I come unglued. "And you didn't bother to mention it?" The question comes out as a screech.

He scrubs a hand through his hair, not meeting my eyes. "Fuck, Holly. We've been going nonstop today. It slipped my mind."

"Damn it, Crey. I've been dreading this shit all day. You could've told me and put me out of my misery."

I pace the room backstage as I rant. I know I'm over-reacting, but Creighton doesn't understand my mama or the stress that comes along with just thinking about her. He watches me pace, letting me vent, which is probably a smart move on his part. Come near the clawing she-beast and you may lose an important appendage, and wouldn't that be a shame?

After about twenty trips back and forth across the fif-teen-foot-wide room, I've calmed down a smidge. I chance a look at where Creighton is leaning against the wall, arms folded over his chest, wondering if he's holding in a laugh for all he's worth. As I stare for a minute, I realize he isn't. But I also can't read what he's thinking.

"What?" I snap. Okay, so the she-beast isn't totally pacified yet. I just need to channel the energy into my performance tonight. *That* I can do.

"You called me Crey," he says.

I shake my head. "Is there something wrong with that?"

He nods slowly. "That's what people close to me call me, but you never have before."

I bite my lip and consider. "So?"

"Nothing. I was surprised, is all." He waves a hand. "Feel free to continue the tirade."

From anyone else it might sound patronizing, but *Crey* just seems to be letting me get it all out. Which is exactly what I need right now. And that realization right there is all it takes to calm me down.

"I'm all tiraded out," I say, stopping in front of him.

"Then maybe this is a good time to ask you if you're up for a flight back to New York after the show next Thursday. I know we haven't really talked about how things are going to work after the tour is over, but I've got some things I need to take care of at home in person that I've been putting off, and I'd like to have you with me."

I've been dreading the *what's next for us* discussion, so my question is tentative. "You get that I don't want to stay in New York permanently?"

Creighton's expression turns serious. "We'll figure it out, Holly."

"Okay. I'll go."

His smile is wide and genuine. "I'm glad I'm not going to have to kidnap you then. I really didn't want to go to the gala alone."

"Gala?"

"A charity thing. At MoMA."

When I open my mouth to say that I'm not sure what MoMA is, he says, "Come here."

I cross the room and stand before him, just out of reach. "We don't have time for anything dirty right about now."

His eyes turn soft in a way I don't remember seeing before. His words are soft too.

"That's not what I want. I just want you in my arms for a minute before the craziness of tonight kicks off."

I close the distance between us and melt against him. The warmth rushing through me from his words turns to molten need when he whispers into my hair.

"But later? Things are going to get as dirty as you can handle." His hand slides down my back and cups my ass, his fingers curling into the crease between my cheeks. "We're going to keep working you up to a bigger plug so I can finally fuck this tight little asshole."

He pulls me against his groin, and the hard, hot length of his cock sends flares of arousal ripping through me when it grinds against my center. I want to dry hump him until I come.

So I do. It takes all of three minutes, with the pressure of his fingers against my ass. Stepping away on shaky legs, I know my cheeks must be flushed, and my hair has to be a disaster.

"I need to go back to Rochelle and Chris to touch up," I whisper.

Creighton's smile is superior, but I'm too content to want to slap it off his face.

"You do that. I'll see you after the meet and greet." His gaze turns sharp. "And don't give Marcus any shit this time about standing so close. He can be out of the picture, but I want him right there in case some fucker tries to make a move on you. Those lips are mine, and I don't share."

He snags my hand, tugs me back close, and pulls me into a kiss before steadying me once again.

I gather myself and then salute. "Sir, yes, sir."

He slaps me on the ass, and I stride out of the room on clicking heels.

CHAPTER
SIXTEEN

Creighton

I'm watching Holly kill her set in Biloxi from what has become my normal place, leaning against a speaker, stage left. From this vantage point, it's clear to me that the arenas are filling sooner at each venue, almost in time with the buzz that has continued to grow in the media about Holly. The stories are focusing more on her and her career now, which is as it should be. People come as curiosity seekers, but even I can tell from the rapt look on their faces that they're leaving as fans.

Right now, Holly has the attention of every single person in the place. People are on their feet, singing along to every single word. Just like every night before, I continue to be in awe of her talent. My wife is a fucking rock star. Well, country star would be more appropriate.

The deep drawl from behind me alerts me to the presence of Boone Thrasher.

"If you keep staring at her like that, you're going to be handing over the keys to your vault, because that woman will know she owns you."

"What are you doing out of your little kingdom before your set?" I ask, glancing at him for only a moment, because I don't want to miss a beat of Holly.

"If you think you're the only one who knows she's a hell of a talent when you see it, then you're wrong. I try to get out here and catch one of her songs every once in a while, but tonight I came out because I had to see for myself that you're just standing here like a smitten kid. People are talkin', you know."

I tear my eyes off Holly to stare him down. "And why would I give a fuck about that?"

"I'm just sayin', the bitch knows she's got you by the balls, you'll have no leverage. And I'm guessing a guy like you is all about leverage."

"What's your point, Thrasher?"

"No point. Just offering a word of wisdom. My woman has me wrapped up pretty neat too, but I don't let her know it."

"I thought you told me I'd better treat her right or you'd be on me?" I vaguely recall his warning from the first day we met, three long days ago.

He cracks the knuckles of his tattooed hand inside the other. "Fuckin' right I will. But that don't mean you gotta be showin' all your cards, man. This is a strategy game, after all."

I laugh, because I feel like I'm the one who should be giving this guy advice. "You ever been married before?"

His chuckle booms out, but the sounds of the bass guitar and drums ensure only I can hear it.

"Nope. That's why I'm giving you advice, Richie Rich. You've already failed at this shit, from what I hear. I'm doing the marriage thing once, and that's it. Thought maybe you'd been all lapdog and pussy whipped before, and that's how you fucked it up. Ladies want to know their man is theirs, but they don't want someone trailin' after 'em like a schoolboy."

"Thanks for the advice, but I think I'm good. You worry about yourself getting pussy-whipped, and I'll worry about Holly."

Thrasher shrugs, but doesn't drop it. "You don't know girls like her, Karas. She's not your high-society type. She's never gonna be easy around your money or your people. Even if she's sipping champagne out of platinum cowboy boots, she'll never lose that backwoods girl. You sure you're okay with that? Because if you're not, it'd be kinder to let her go now before she falls for you."

There are so many responses I can give to what he just said, but I don't reply because I'm stuck on his last words. *"Before she falls for you."* Because she hasn't yet.

It's a sobering reality check. I've decided what we have is the real thing, and Holly . . . I have no frigging clue what she thinks. The only place she'll let her guard down is in the bedroom—or wherever we happen to be when I'm giving her every bit of pleasure she can handle. I know how to seduce my wife, but how the hell do I break down her walls? How do I get her to trust me?

"Oh shit!" Thrasher yells as a fan throws himself on-stage only a few feet from where Holly stands. I lunge forward, but Thrasher grabs my arm. "No, man, not your fight this time."

Security is on the guy before he can reach his finger-tips out to touch the toe of her boots, and he's dragged away.

Holly barely misses a beat, finishing the last chorus of the song while the band plays on. When the music finally quiets, she speaks into her microphone. "Well, I guess he really liked that one, didn't he, ya'll?" The crowd cheers even louder, and she flashes a wide smile and launches into the final song on the set list.

I shake off Thrasher's arm and turn to him. "Don't you ever try to get between me and Holly. You get me, Thrash-er? Not here, not anywhere."

My tone promises violence, as my rage at his interfer-ence pulses to the surface. She's my woman. I will fucking protect her from everyone and everything.

Thrasher just shakes his head. "You've got a lot to learn, man, especially about her. She's a strong woman. She doesn't need you to save her. Hell, she found a way to use you to save herself. Don't ever underestimate her be-cause it'll be the biggest mistake you make, I can promise you that. Country girls got grit like you couldn't imagine."

"You think I don't know she's fucking special?" I ges-ture to the stage. "She's a goddamn goddess out there, and I'd have to be blind to miss it."

Thrasher nods. "Good, and don't you fucking forget

it." He turns to walk back toward the hallway that leads to his designated room, and then pauses. "You should both come out with us tonight. We're gonna hit up one of my favorite bars. Play some horseshoes in the pits out back. Let's see if you can hang with the country boys."

The last thing I want to do tonight is go out and hang with this cocky punk who thinks he knows more about Holly than I do, but something keeps me from saying no. Instead, I punt.

"I'll leave that up to Holly."

"Pussy-whipped motherfucker."

The words are tossed over Thrasher's shoulder, and I flip off his back as he walks away. I don't like the son of a bitch, but then again, I don't exactly hate him either. He's looking out for Holly, and that I have to respect.

But horseshoes? Really?

CHAPTER
SEVENTEEN

Holly

"She's kicking your ass, man!"

"You're on his team, which means she's kicking your ass too!"

The guys in my band are getting no end of amusement from ribbing the crap out of Creighton during our game of horseshoes at Boone's favorite bar outside Biloxi. I couldn't believe it when Creighton deferred to me about whether or not we join them rather than scooping me up and carrying me off to the bus, like he did the other nights after I finished up "That Girl" during Boone's set.

Tonight, Creighton was waiting offstage with a beer and a smile. The beer was his, because I was still on the "tour diet from hell," but he handed it over anyway and told me that Boone invited us out and he was leaving it up to me to decide.

In all honesty, my lady parts kind of need a break from the nonstop banging that we've been doing, and after-show sex is turning into the most energetic kind. So I said yes, partially out of self-preservation.

Now I'm wondering if I made the right choice. Creighton isn't exactly showing any signs of wanting to commit murder, though. He's just sipping on a beer and shrugging off the comments.

Finally, he says, "Since my ass is hers, she can kick it whenever she wants."

His words come just as I'm swinging to toss my horseshoe and the throw goes wild, nearly kneecapping Boone.

He jumps back out of the way, his beer splashing out of the bar's trademark red Solo cups. "Shit, woman. Watch your throw!"

But I'm not paying attention to Boone. I couldn't care less about him, his kneecaps, or his beer. I'm staring at Creighton, trying to interpret what that comment meant. *My ass is hers.*

Is he truly in this for real? I mean, he's said that I'm his, but it's never really been a mutual sort of ownership like you'd have in a "real" marriage. Or is living in the middle of a tour, where we've finally found our rhythm, messing with his head?

All I know is that I'm scared to hope that this might last. Hope is a dangerous thing, and when it comes to Creighton, I'm terrified to gamble everything. This man has the power to wreck me.

Even as the thoughts circle my brain and I reach for

the next horseshoe, I know I'm full of crap. It's already too late. I've placed my bet, and it's my heart that's on the line.

CHAPTER EIGHTEEN

Creighton

A week later

It almost feels strange to know that I'm not getting back on a tour bus in a few hours. I can honestly say this has been a fascinating experience. Ten days, seven cities, and the constant reinforcement that I'm married to a woman of incredible talent. Experiencing Holly in her element has been eye-opening. She's got grit and drive, and works harder than my hardest-working executive.

But as confident and bold as she's been on tour, the moment we landed in New York City this morning, she drew into herself and uncertainty bloomed. I just need to close the deal, get this charity thing out of the way, and then I'll be able to get her accustomed to this part of her life, her future. I need her to be comfortable here, because if I get my way, we'll split our time between New York and wherever she needs to be. Wherever *she* chooses to be.

My pen hovers over the signature line of the document that will ensure no one will ever dictate to Holly again about her career. Never again will anyone have that kind of power over her.

I scrawl my signature on the line, and it's done. Homegrown Records is mine.

We agreed to the initial terms of the deal the day Holly walked out on me in New York. I was so caught up in negotiations that I didn't stop to take her call. Those negotiations were critical, heavily featuring her and her contract, and the fact that during the weeks between signing and closing, the execs couldn't do a goddamn thing that would negatively affect her. It was a rookie husband mistake that almost cost me more than losing the deal would have.

But having both of those fuckers at the table in front of me brought out a protective side of me I never knew existed. With every snide comment about how they lifted Holly out of some sad existence and gave her a shot through their show, I grew more and more determined to have their resignations in my hand.

She was a girl who didn't know better and had nothing to lose when she signed their heavy-handed agreement. Knowing Holly now, they could have put anything in that contract, and she would have agreed to it just to have a shot at her dream. The fact that they continued to jerk her around with the JC situation was unconscionable. They deserved to be tossed out of the industry, in my opinion.

"Hope you know what you're doin', boy."

I look up at Morty, the paunchy executive I'm tempted to have blackballed from the industry starting today. His threats over what he could do to Holly's career had me wanting to rip his throat from his neck during negotiations. The fact that he's trying to bait me just shows what an idiot he is.

"He doesn't have a clue what he's doin'," Jim, Morty's sidekick, says. "All he knows is this is the surest way to own that woman lock, stock, and barrel. You think she's going to be happy that you did this? Mark my words, she'll want your balls in a sling."

I pin them both with a glare that would have smarter men shaking in their fancy, spit-shined cowboy boots. "You're dead fucking wrong about my motivations, and if I gave a shit what you thought, I'd correct you. But since I don't, I think it's time you hand over those resignations and get on your way."

I shove the final documents aside, not concerned in the slightest about his prediction. Holly will understand that this has nothing to do with ownership or control, and everything to do with setting her free from these pricks who've been running her life. And if she doesn't get that, then I'll help her understand.

The men stand, Morty glaring daggers at me and Jim looking amused, but I don't give a fuck. I don't waste another thought on them as they exit the room. I just want to go home, kick back on the couch with my wife in my lap and a beer in my hand, but that can't happen anytime soon, thanks to the charity event I've committed us to.

Once the room clears of lawyers and the former record execs, Cannon and I are left alone. He wastes no time.

"Well, Crey, I think you got a hell of a deal, but I don't think you know what you're doing either. We have to learn this industry from the bottom up, and we only scratched the surface during diligence."

He's been on hand to sign several of the documents in his capacity as vice president of the new entity I formed for the sole purpose of this acquisition. One not under the umbrella of Karas International, like all of my other companies. One that I own one hundred percent of personally, because never before has an acquisition been this personal to me.

"Is that supposed to be news to me?"

"I'm just saying—"

"Everything you've already said before. And it's getting old." I rise out of the leather conference room chair and tuck my pen into the inside pocket of my suit jacket. "I have a beautiful woman waiting for me, and if I get home in time, she might still be strolling around the house in her lingerie."

Cannon smirks at me. "Now there's a thought."

"Get it out of your fucking brain."

He holds both hands up in a pacifying gesture. "Jeez. I'm just fucking with you, Crey. No different from what we've always done."

I stiffen when I realize that even my best friend doesn't get it. "She's different. Everything about this is different."

"Come on. You didn't even know the woman when you posted that ludicrous ad. It's only been a couple of weeks. There's no way in hell you can know that it's *different*."

There have been several times in the past when Cannon and I haven't seen eye to eye. If we can't settle things with a logical discussion, we usually opt for beating the shit out of each other in a boxing ring. I open my mouth to argue, but snap it shut just as quickly.

I don't need to justify this to him; I don't even need his fucking support. I know what I've got with Holly, and that's not changing, even if his opinion doesn't.

I turn and leave the room with his confused "What the fuck, man?" following me out.

CHAPTER
NINETEEN

Creighton

Holly is already wearing her dress for the charity event when I enter the bedroom. She's absolutely breathtaking, and I can't get over what a lucky son of a bitch I am.

If sex could be painted on a body, that's what this dress would be. Red satin, hugging her every curve from her shoulders to just below her knees before it flares into a little mermaid-looking thing. I have no earthly idea how the fuck she's going to walk in it, but I don't care. I'll fucking carry her.

She's surveying herself in the mirror when her eyes dart to mine in the reflection.

"What do you think? Should I wear the black one?" She motions to the long black dress hanging from the valet rod in the closet.

"Don't you dare take that dress off."

Her eyes snap back to mine. "Wha—"

I close in behind her, reaching into my pocket to pull out the gift I purchased at Harry Winston earlier in the day. I bring my arms around her, letting the diamond collar rest against her neck.

Her chest rises and falls as she looks in the mirror. "Holy. Shit. Please tell me those are CZs."

"Afraid I can't do that, babe."

Her eyes widen so much that I'm a little worried she's going to hurt herself. She lifts a hand to her neck after I engage the clasp, but her fingers stop short of touching the diamonds.

"It's not going to bite."

She spins around to face me. "Please tell me it's rented only for tonight, and you're taking it back tomorrow."

"Afraid I can't do that either."

"You have to take it back."

Now the conversation is growing tedious. "It's not going anywhere but around your neck."

"Why in God's name would you spend that kind of money on me?"

"Because I can."

"Are you trying to make me feel like Julia Roberts in *Pretty Woman*?"

I look at her, confusion flooding me. "What are you talking about?"

"The movie. *Pretty Woman*. She's a hooker and he's a millionaire. There's this scene with a necklace. It's pretty freaking famous, Crey."

"I don't see the comparison. You're not a hooker; you're my wife. I can buy you whatever the hell I want. That's my right," I say.

To myself I add, *Including a fucking record label.*

Holly slips around me and stalks to the floor-to-ceiling windows. Pressing a hand to the glass, she stares down at the lights of the city and off toward Central Park.

I follow her. "It's only money, Holly. I've got plenty. If I want to spoil you, I will."

Once again I'm taking in her reflection, but this time, there are tears running down her face.

"Whoa. Why the tears?" I lay my hands on her shoulders and turn her to face me. My thumbs catch the drops as they fall. "If you hate it that much, we can get you something different."

Holly reaches up and moves my hands away from her face before using the side of her index finger to swipe away the remaining moisture without destroying her makeup.

"God, I'm sorry. I'm a frigging disaster."

"You're beautiful. As soon as I saw you standing in front of that mirror, I knew I'd never seen a more beautiful woman in my life."

Her lips wobble into a sad smile. "And here I was looking in the mirror, thinking that the only thing that would make this dress more perfect would be my gran's pearls that my gramps brought her home from Japan after the war." Her smile falters and disappears. "But that can never happen now."

"Why not?"

"Because the sheriff called to tell me that apparently

when they picked Mama up for her B&E, it was actually her second trip into Gran's house, and she'd apparently just come back from the pawn shop."

"What did she take?" I ask, hating Holly's tears and the crazy feeling of helplessness they give me. Whatever her mom took, I'll get it back if the police haven't already.

"From what the pawnbroker said, most or all of Gran's jewelry. The jewelry that I was too careless to get a safe deposit box to store because I assumed it was safe locked up and hidden in her house. But Mama knew where the special hiding spots were, and she wasn't shy about snatching it. She probably thought she was entitled to it anyway. She was her mama, after all."

"So if the pawnbroker reported it to the police, then they recovered it already?" Confusion edges my tone because I feel like I'm missing something here.

Holly shakes her head. "No, the pawnbroker didn't realize it was stolen until he heard about my mama being arrested today when he was at bowling league. He sold her locket, her earrings, and the pearl necklace."

My confusion gives way to anger. "Shouldn't he be held responsible by the police? They have an obligation to hold things for a period of time to ensure they're not stolen, I thought." I don't know the ins and outs of the pawn business, but I would assume that's the smartest choice.

Once again, Holly's face falls. "He didn't even consider it was a possibility. My mama probably sold him some line of bull. I don't know. But they're gone."

"I'm sorry, baby."

"Gran was the first person in my life to actually give

a shit about me, and I feel like I've failed her again." Her whole body is racked with shudders.

"Holly—" I say, trying to interrupt and calm her down, but she doesn't stop.

"It's not about the jewelry, that's just one more example of how many bad decisions I've made. Leaving her with my mama to go on the show . . . that was the ultimate mistake. *I* made that choice. *I* decided to take my one shot. And it cost me *everything* that mattered. When am I going to stop messing up?" She turns and presses her palms against the glass again.

I step behind her and wrap my arms around her middle, pulling her back into my body. I want to hold her up, infuse her with my strength.

I hate seeing this strong woman edge toward breaking. The first time she told me the story about her grandmother and what happened, I watched from the sidelines while Holly grieved. I'm not willing to remain on the sidelines ever again when it comes to her.

"I'm so *fucking* sorry, baby. I wish I could go back and change it all for you. If I had the power to do that, I would." My words are rusty and harsh, coming from a place deep inside me never touched before Holly.

Her body relaxes into me for a beat before she straightens. "It's something I have to live with. The best tribute I can give her is to succeed, to make her proud."

She turns to face me, and I can almost see her pulling the layers of her armor back over herself. As much as I hate seeing her raw like this, there's something almost heart-stopping about having a window into her soul.

When her dark brown eyes shutter, I hate that even more.

"I better go fix my face if we're going to make it on time."

"We don't have to go." I'm not willing to skip the event to indulge myself, but when it comes to Holly, I'm willing to break all my own rules.

She twists out of my hold, shaking her head. "I'll be fine. Besides, it won't be the last time I lose it over this. It's something I have to live with for the rest of my life. We all have to make choices; I just didn't know that I'd be losing the only person who will ever care about me that much. Life's a bitch that way."

The whole time she's speaking, she's walking backward across the room, and with her final declaration, she disappears from my sight, down the hallway toward the master suite.

But her words still hang in the air, haunting me and taunting me in equal measure. I have more money than I can spend in five lifetimes, but I can't give Holly the one thing she desperately wants. It's a forcefully humbling reality.

The next thought that flashes through my brain is equally sobering.

She's wrong.

Her gran is not the only person who will ever care about her that much.

CHAPTER
TWENTY

Holly

I sip my glass of champagne and survey the moneyed crowd filling the Museum of Modern Art. After my breakdown earlier, I had to completely redo my makeup. Nothing like a couple of swipes of foundation and concealer to cover the layers of grief and guilt.

Too bad it can't hide my country girl awkwardness at attending an event that's so far out of my league. The last thing I want to do tonight is screw up and make some social blunder that will embarrass Creighton and end up in the papers.

I skim over the crowd, taking in the dark-hued designer dresses and diamonds that aren't as flashy as the ones around my neck. I wasn't sure what to expect of this thing, but now that we've been here for ten minutes, I've recognized more faces than I ever would have expected.

There must be at least a hundred people here who are more famous than me, not that I consider myself actually famous at all. The number of them who probably knew who I was—*before* Creighton married me? I'm guessing that number is in the single digits.

Not too many good ole boys who are used to sitting on tailgates with a beer in one hand and a spit bottle in the other, that's for sure. I think it's also safe to say there is no overlap in this crowd with the *Country Dreams* target demographic.

In other words, I'm completely out of my depth. Even after being in the public eye for months, this kind of situation unnerves me. I'm much more at home on a stage in front of my kind of people. People who want to listen to music that tells stories about people just like them. Instead, I'm standing at an event that costs about the same as a brand-new S-10 pickup to attend.

It doesn't help that I can't get Garth Brooks's "Friends in Low Places" out of my head. At least I made it past the cameras outside the entrance without incident. That was something.

The walkway was covered with a fine dusting of snow, and I was positive that I'd bite it if I didn't cling to Creighton's arm like a drunk monkey. So cling, I did.

And then I nabbed a glass of champagne from a passing server's tray at the first opportunity. Liquid courage. I need a lot more of it in order to get through tonight.

For the first time since I married Creighton, I feel like arm candy. That's not to say that Creighton has given me any reason to feel like that, but I can't help it. He introduced me and tried to include me in conversation, but my answers were awkward and short.

I need to get my shit together so I can fool them and make him proud. Maybe I can hire one of those acting coaches and learn to bluff my way through things like this? It's never going to come naturally to me. I just don't belong in this crowd.

And from the stares of the women that dart away as soon as I accidentally make eye contact, it's clear they know I don't belong either. I can just imagine what they're whispering as they tilt their heads toward one another.

Yes, she's the girl he married after a one-night stand. Do you think he had any idea she would be so out of place?

Or *I bet he's wishing he'd stuck to his own kind.*

Or maybe even, *I'll be ready to swoop in once he's bored with her.*

In their black dresses, they look like a flock of crows just waiting to swoop in on the carnage they expect my marriage with Creighton to become.

On any other day, I'd like to think this would strengthen my resolve to prove them wrong, but tonight, I'm feeling too raw, and it's a fight just to conceal my weaknesses.

Creighton shakes hands and talks business with several more people, and I keep clinging and smiling. I don't understand what the hell they're talking about, and my cheeks already hurt. We've only been here for twenty minutes, and already I can't wait to leave.

I force my anxieties away. I'm here because this is important to Creighton. I listen with half an ear as the conversation turns to some new investment that a close-talking guy in a tux and red plaid bowtie thinks Creighton should invest in.

I wait for the guy to take a breath, and squeeze Creighton's arm. His attention shifts to me immediately, his dark eyes soft and . . . affectionate?

A wave of warmth slides through me, and for the first time since we climbed out of the limo, I'm not completely on edge and miserable. I need to learn to be comfortable by his side while he shines in his own spotlight. He's a compelling man and I'm proud that he's mine, but I have so much to learn before I'll ever be confident in his world.

I clear my throat quietly to interrupt the close talker. "I'm going to excuse myself for a moment. I need to freshen up."

Proud of myself, I mentally pat myself on the back for using a ladylike term rather than saying something like *I'm going to take a piss.* Considering the company I've been keeping for the past few weeks—like Boone and my band and the roadies—I probably deserve bonus points for that one.

I slip my hand from where it's been clutching his arm—good Lord, I think I left a sweaty handprint on his tux—but Creighton grabs it before I can withdraw it completely. He turns toward me, ignoring the now silent man, and uses my hand to pull me closer. He places his half-full drink on the tray of a passing waiter, and lifts his other hand to my face.

I watch the liquor as it's carried away, unsure what the hell Creighton is doing. PDA? I didn't think he was the type, and I'm certainly not. My thoughts stall as he lowers his head to my ear.

"If I promise to stop talking about boring shit, will you promise to hurry back?"

I smile at his request. Leave it to Creighton to say something to make me feel a little less out of place.

"If I don't get lost."

"Good enough." His lips graze the very spot his breath just touched.

I step back, my eyes darting up to his. The warmth and affection are still burning in them.

As I walk away from the safety of his presence, a feeling of unease fills my chest.

CHAPTER
TWENTY-ONE

Holly

Once I leave the ladies' room, I take my time making my way back to Creighton. It's not intentional, I just keep getting distracted by all the cool exhibits. Who wouldn't? It's not like I've been here before, but I definitely plan to come back.

I pause in front of a piece of artwork on the wall that's all wire and metal music notes. It sings to me. Given that music is my life, I can't help but be drawn to it—and it's not crazy ugly like some of the things I've seen tonight.

"Lovely, isn't it?"

I turn to see a gorgeous woman with white-blond hair and a striking Kelly-green silk dress clinging to her every curve. Her boobs may be fake, but if they are, they're the expensive kind of fake that makes it hard to tell. I feel like

Meghan March

a guy checking out her rack and drag my eyes up to hers. Vivid green, just like the dress.

She doesn't seem to notice my minor detour because she's studying me in turn. Her eyes don't catch on my chest, but on the necklace.

"Well, Creighton's certainly gotten more generous. That Harry Winston is to die for."

I can't read her tone. She doesn't sound catty, but . . . something else.

"Thank you."

She holds out a hand, and I can't help but notice her perfect manicure. "I'm Annika Frederickson."

We shake hands, and I open my mouth to say my name, but she beats me to it. "And you're Holly Wix Karas."

I think it's interesting that she tacks the *Karas* part on, but I'm not going to dispute it. It's just that most people who recognize me wouldn't think to do that. But something tells me that she doesn't recognize me from CMT, because I can't picture her watching that channel, and on top of that, she already mentioned Creighton. She's obviously part of his circle.

"It's nice to meet you." I release her hand and turn halfway toward the door. "I should probably be getting back."

She nods politely, and I'm a dozen feet away when she says, "I hope the third time's truly a charm for Creighton. Does that three-strikes rule apply to marriages? I suppose not, considering how many men and women I know are on husband or wife number four or five."

My body freezes, but my brain races, repeating her

148

words over and over. The blood rushing in my ears drowns out the noise from the crowded event only a hundred feet away.

Third time's a charm? Three strikes?

What. The. Hell. We had the ex-wife discussion, and Creighton told me about Shaw.

I smooth over my shock and turn back toward Annika. Her head is tilted toward me, as if she's waiting for some kind of reaction.

I'm doing everything I can to keep from giving her one beyond saying, "I don't know who you think you are—"

She smiles, condescension practically radiating brighter than her perfectly white teeth. "Because I suppose I didn't introduce myself properly." She holds out her hand again. This time her perfect nails look like claws.

"Annika Mitchell Karas Frederickson. I believe you could call me the original Mrs. Karas."

I don't shake her hand this time. I just stand there dumbly, in who-knows-how many hundreds of thousands of dollars worth of diamonds, and stare at this woman. Now I see the calculating gleam in her eyes, and I have no idea how I missed it before.

"Oh, I take it he didn't tell you about me. Not surprising. It must still be painful for him to talk about. I was the one who left him, after all."

I'm blinking rapidly, trying to take in what she's saying. "When? When were you married?"

"Years ago. But there are some wounds that never heal. I can't say that I don't regret my rashness to end it. We were both so young, so in love."

I snort. "You couldn't have been that in love if you left him."

Her sly smile fades a degree. "Sometimes you have to let go of the one you love, even if it's not what you truly want."

"Why are you telling me this?"

"Because I think you should know what kind of man you're married to. From what I can tell, and from what wife number two has shared with me, he hasn't changed a bit."

"What? You're going to tell me he's kinky?" I smirk. "Sorry, honey. Too late. I already figured that one out."

"No. But I'm glad to see you enjoy being treated like a plaything. Because that's all you'll ever truly be. A toy. Something to be enjoyed and displayed when he needs you, and then tucked away or bought off when he's done with you."

Annika looks around the museum and then back at me, her gaze landing on the necklace. "Isn't that what he's doing tonight? Playing dress-up with you and bringing you out to show you off? Have you done anything tonight beyond hanging on his arm? Made any scintillating contributions to his endless business discussions? Or have you just been a pretty accessory?"

Catfight levels of rage are rising within me, held only in check by the small part of me that whispers, *You know there's some truth to what she says.* It's like the woman poked around in my brain and latched onto my biggest fear.

Well, screw her. I can smell a shit stirrer . . . but in her case, what she's stirring is the truth. Still, I don't need to listen to this. Letting someone talk crap about Creighton to my face ain't gonna fly.

"You listen here—"

"No," she says quickly. "You listen. If you think for one minute that he's going to want you for longer than you serve as that pretty accessory, then you're delusional. He'll never love you. I had everything in common with him— same schools, same friends, same social status, same hobbies—and there was nothing I could do to draw him away from his first love. Winning."

Her eyes gleaming, she says, "He needs the rush. He's an adrenaline junkie, but instead of getting his kicks from jumping out of airplanes, he gets them by checking yet another goal off his list. That stunt with the missed connection? A rather unique ploy for him to find you after a one-night stand because you piqued his curiosity. But do you really think you'll satisfy him for long? You have nothing in common. You're not even from the same social stratosphere. He's probably lucky you didn't speak tonight because that hillbilly twang of yours would draw attention to just how backwoods you really are. It might be quaint when you're doing an interview on country radio, but in Creighton's world, you're nothing but a liability."

The blood rushing through my ears is back full force. I have no idea what she has to gain by flinging these hateful words at me, but she must have some motive.

I pretend I'm onstage after I've just messed up a lyric, and I push through, smoothing a smile on my face so no one will notice that I'm cringing inside at my mistake.

"Why are you telling me this? What reason could you possibly have?"

Annika lifts her chin, and I don't know if her nose can get any higher in the air. "Consider it my public service announcement. I left him because I refused to be marginalized. You've got a good thing going with that country music shtick. I can only imagine it's exactly what you've wanted since you were a little girl sitting in the trailer park listening to the radio in some broken-down car propped up on blocks."

I wince. I don't know where she got that image, but she's altogether too close to the truth for comfort.

"And?" I prompt. I'm not willing to let her see me cower.

"And I thought, as a woman who's known Creighton for twenty years, you'd want to know exactly what you're getting in to. If you think it's worth giving up your dreams, you might want to reassess. Because for girls like you," she points her finger at me, as if I need to know who she's talking about, "if you don't jump on your once-in-a-lifetime chance, you may never get another one. If I were you, I'd do some serious thinking about whether it was my dream career or a man I should be chasing harder."

My heart thuds in my chest when she lays it out so baldly. I have no idea why she thinks it's her place to tell me this, but I've heard enough.

"Thanks for the warning. I think we're done here."

Annika smiles, all grace and elegance again. Not a single trace of malice to be found. "It was lovely to meet you, Holly. I hear you've got a great shot at the New Artist

Award this year. Best of luck." And with that, she turns, green dress swirling around her ankles, and makes the best exit I've ever seen outside of a movie.

I, on the other hand, want to sink into the exhibit chair, curl up into a ball, and lick the wounds she's left me with.

She has to have a motive for her words; she would never bother with me if she didn't. But do her motives really matter? Even if everything she said was bull, it's nothing I haven't thought myself.

It's time for me to face facts. Fact number one, I'm falling for Creighton. Skip falling, I've *fallen*. It's the first time I've acknowledged how deep I've gotten into this, and I swallow back the gut-wrenching fear it produces. Because what if she's right? What if he gets bored as soon as the lipstick on the pig that's me rubs off?

Absently staring at the beautiful works of art surrounding me, I wonder if this is how my future with him will always be. Evening after evening where I'm seen and not heard, and the only talent required of me is hanging off his arm without making a scene.

Is that all I have to look forward to as part of his life? That isn't what I signed up for. I need to think, somewhere I'm not second-guessing every single move I make.

The crushing weight of everything—the grief and guilt and confusion and pressure and stress—bears down on me until my breathing shallows and dizziness hits me. I've felt off all night after my earlier breakdown, and now my forehead goes clammy and I stumble backward until I hit the wall and slide down it, not caring about the dress or how ridiculous I must look. I drop my head back against the wall, trying to breathe, but I just can't get enough air into my lungs.

"Whoa. Are you okay? Shit. You don't look so good."

I don't recognize the voice, and I don't care. All I care about is trying to get enough oxygen into my body so I don't pass out on this fancy floor.

The man barks out Creighton's name. I don't know how much time passes—it could be seconds or minutes or hours, but soon Creighton is crouching beside me, pressing my head between my knees, and saying softly, "Breathe, Holly. Just breathe. Slow down."

I try to slow my breathing as he's directed, trying to match him as he inhales and exhales. Eventually the clawing in my lungs subsides, and I raise my head slowly and stare into concerned brown eyes.

"Are you okay? What the hell happened?"

His soothing tone evaporates. His questions are sharp and demanding. My breathing picks up speed again.

"Oh shit. Calm down, Holly. I'm sorry. I shouldn't have . . . Let's get you out of here."

He reaches an arm behind my back, and I know he's going to pick me up and carry me out of the museum. I'll look like a complete idiot to everyone in attendance, and that's not even including the pictures that will end up on the Internet. The next thing you know, *TMZ* will say I fainted because I'm pregnant, and I'll be on baby-bump watch for the next six months.

I push his hand away. "I can walk."

Creighton's gaze narrows, but he holds out a hand and

helps me to my feet.

"Are you sure?"

I nod. "Let's go."

CHAPTER
TWENTY-TWO

Holly

I've barely gotten out of my dress and into a comfy T-shirt and pajama pants before Creighton knocks on the bedroom door.

The knocking throws me. He's never done that before. The reason for it becomes apparent when the door swings open, and he walks in with a man I've never seen before.

I look sharply at Creighton. "Um . . . what's going on?"

"This is Dr. Wylie. He's my personal physician. I asked him to come check you out."

Of course he did, and without even bothering to ask me if I need a doctor. Too bad Dr. Wylie made an unnecessary trip.

"I'm good, thanks."

Creighton glances at the doctor and then back at me.

"A moment, if you would." Dr. Wylie nods and steps out of the room, and Creighton closes the door. "He's checking you out, and I don't care what arguments you give me."

"It's not necessary."

Creighton shoves his hands through his dark hair. "You fucking collapsed in the middle of MoMA. Don't tell me it's not necessary."

"I'm fine."

"You obviously aren't fine. And if you can't tell me what the fuck happened, Dr. Wylie is checking you out."

Tell him what happened? I don't have a fucking clue what happened, so it's not like I can give Creighton the explanation he's looking for. And I'm sure as hell not ready to tell him about my encounter with his *other* ex-wife. So I guess the doctor is checking me out.

"Fine. It's not like anything I say is going to make a difference. You might as well send him in."

I sit on the end of the bed, knowing I'm acting like a spoiled brat, but I want to get this over with so I can go to bed. I just need sleep and the dawn of a new day to see things clearly. I need to put some time and space between me and the things Annika said tonight. Her name burns on my tongue, and I'm dying to confront him.

Why didn't he tell me about her? Was she the one who got away? I shake my head, trying unsuccessfully to dislodge the thoughts.

"What is going on, Holly? This isn't like you at all."

My head snaps up. "All of a sudden you know me so well?" Too bad I can't say the same about him.

His face twists into a frustrated, bemused expression.

157

It's like he's looking at me and there's a sign above my head that says Unbalanced woman. Treat with more caution than homemade dynamite.

Just when I think he's going to let my jab pass without comment, he says quietly, as if to himself and not to me, "I thought I did. Maybe I was wrong."

I feel a pang in my chest, but refuse to acknowledge it.

"Send him in then. I just want to go to bed."

Creighton's dark gaze burns into me. "If that's what you want. But don't think that means this subject is closed for good. You scared the shit out of me."

"And almost embarrassed you too," I add.

He just shakes his head, brow furrowed. "I'll send in Dr. Wylie. I've got some calls to make, so don't wait up."

Creighton apparently lied, because Dr. Wylie just left, and he's hovering in the doorway. I can't read him. I don't want to read him. I just want to close my eyes and forget about everything that happened tonight, but that's not in the cards.

Creighton crosses the room and sits on the edge of the bed. His suit jacket is gone, and his shirt is open at the collar, exposing his corded neck. His sleeves are rolled up to his elbows, and his hands grip his knees.

He studies me for long moments before asking, "You want to tell me what the hell happened tonight?"

"Not particularly."

"Then I'll rephrase. *Tell me* what the fuck happened

tonight."

He's losing patience with me. I should care more, but I'm not the one with ex-wives popping out of the woodwork.

"Or what?" I counter.

He releases one knee and brings his arm up, his hand shoving through his hair.

"What the hell is going on with you? Something happened. Because all of a sudden you're not . . . Holly."

Fuck it. If he wants to push, I'll tell him.

"I met someone tonight."

His face is expressionless when he says, "Go on."

I pull my knees up and wrap my arms around them, the same way I used to when I sat on Gran's bed to tell her about school.

"Why didn't you tell me I'm number three?" I ask, my voice completely devoid of emotion.

Creighton goes very still. "Who told you about Annika?"

"What I want to know is why *you* didn't."

"Who told you?" he repeats, his tone hard.

I drop my arms and shove myself up the bed so I'm leaning against the headboard, arms crossed in front of me.

"Annika told me about Annika."

Creighton lifts his other hand and rubs the side of his face. "Fuck."

"Why didn't you tell me?"

"I agree with you. This conversation is best saved for tomorrow."

Oh, hell no.

"I don't think so. You're the one who wanted to know. So now you know. Why didn't you tell me? You told me about Shaw—why not Annika?"

He rises up from the bed and begins pacing the room. His back is to me when he says, "Because it wasn't important."

I blink, trying to comprehend what he just said. *She was his wife. How is it possible that wasn't important?*

"It sounds pretty fucking important to me."

He turns and paces back toward me. His mouth is pressed into a thin, tense line. "I was young and stupid. It doesn't matter anymore. It has absolutely no bearing on our marriage."

I'm processing his words and not liking them one bit. How can a marriage *not matter*. You don't marry someone who doesn't matter . . . unless you're marrying the woman you had a one-night stand with but can't find again.

"Is that what you're going to tell wife number four about me? That it was just some stupid stunt and was fun for a while, but it doesn't matter anymore?"

"What are you talking about, Holly?"

"You just told me that you married a woman, presumably loved her, and now she's not even worth a mention. I'm just trying to figure out how women rate in your life after they've outlived their usefulness to you."

"You're being unreasonable," he growls. "It was a long time ago. I didn't love her. It was a whim."

I cluck my tongue. "Good to know she and I have more in common than I thought."

His jaw is clenched so tight, I'm almost positive he's going to start breaking teeth. Finally, he bites out, "You have nothing in common with Annika. Not one fucking thing."

All the blood drains from my face, and I'm freezing, even though I'm surrounded by a warm pile of blankets.

"You're right. *She* had everything in common with you, and *she* was kind enough to point out that I have nothing in common with you and am just a toy to be played with while I'm new and shiny. I'm surprised she didn't sticker me with an expiration date. Although, I hear they're taking odds on that in Vegas."

Creighton winces. "That's not what I fucking meant. Don't twist my words around."

The words are flowing now, and I can't stop them. "I'm just taking them at face value, *Crey*. Do you have any other ex-wives hiding in the wings I need to know about? Any secret children or mistresses you don't think are important?"

His nostrils flare and the muscle ticks in his jaw. I can sense the moment when I've officially pushed him too far.

CHAPTER TWENTY-THREE

Creighton

I'm staring at the woman I'm in love with—that's right, fucking in love with—and in the space of a heartbeat, I realize she doesn't feel the same way about me. Maybe she never will.

Pain claws through my chest, matching the fear that tore through me when someone came running to get me after she collapsed at MoMA. Her every breath matters to me more than my own, and she's completely oblivious.

She's also oblivious to the fact that she's finding my breaking point. Years of trying to earn someone's love and being met with contempt at every turn grips my throat like a stranglehold. I lost my parents to a horrific attack, and instead of being welcomed into a family that would love and accept and comfort me, I walked into completely the opposite, into the care of someone devoid of any feelings that would help a grieving boy deal with the loss of his parents.

Even after everything, Holly doesn't trust me. Objectively I know I should have told her about Annika, but that is my own private failure, and compared to what I feel for Holly, Annika is completely inconsequential and meaningless. It's like trying to compare a raindrop to a hurricane.

My words strike like lashes, and the driving force behind them is the knowledge that whatever I thought we were building is nothing but a figment of my imagination.

"If you're looking for a reason to get out of this, Holly, I'm sure you can find one. I'm not going to beg you to stay."

Her face hardens into a nearly unrecognizable mask, and I wait for the cracks to show at my words.

But I get nothing except silence.

I'm not going to beg for her affection. Holly's made it clear that she can't be bought, and apparently I'm not deserving of it through my actions.

I watch her face, eyes riveted, waiting for a single hint that there's something to fight for, but right now, she might as well be a stranger to me.

My temper is yanking on its chain, and I know I need to leave before I say something I can never take back.

I turn on my heel and head for the door. My steps are measured, and all I want from her is a single word. Maybe two.

Don't go, I want her to say.
But she says nothing.
And I'm gone.

CHAPTER
TWENTY-FOUR

Holly

Pride is a dangerous thing, but when it's all you have left, how do you make yourself let go of it?

Hours later, I'm still curled up in the mammoth bed alone. I shift my face away from the wet spot on my pillow, refusing to acknowledge that I've soaked it with my tears.

When did my life get so complicated? Oh yeah, when I decided to marry a guy I only met once—and by met, I mean banged until I could barely walk.

I think about what Dr. Wylie told me. His diagnosis: panic attack, caused by stress. His prescription: take some time to relax and get away from the stress.

It's thinking about that last part that caused the tears to start running.

I can't stay in New York, but I don't want to go back

to Nashville.

There's only one place I can think to go.

Home.

It echoes in my head as I finally fall asleep.

Creighton never comes back. When I open my eyes at seven a.m., his side of the bed is empty and still neatly made, no impressions in the pillow. I wonder if he ever even came back to the penthouse. I pull on a sweatshirt and socks, and go investigate.

It's still expensive, perfect, and completely unwelcoming.

I don't belong here. The panic starts to rise again. It's sharp and fast, stealing any rational thought. Words flash back through my brain like they're lit with neon.

"It wasn't important."

"It was a whim."

"You're nothing like Annika."

The slam of the door.

I don't belong here.

Then a new phrase pierces through on a continuous loop.

I have to get out of here. I have to get out of here. I have to get out of here.

The words drown out every other thought until I find myself in my closet, tossing on the first thing I grab before shoving clothes into a bag. I stumble into the bathroom and grab random shit off the counter and from the drawers until my suitcase is full. I don't know what I've packed. I don't care.

I have to get out of here.

I rush through the living room and into the kitchen, spying the same damn notepad I used before.

Creighton's going to want to kill me when he gets home.

But I'll already be gone.

I scrawl the same two words, but this time for an entirely different reason.

Good-bye, Creighton.

Holly and Creighton's story concludes in *Dirty Together*.

You know you don't want to miss what's coming next! Click here (http://www.meghanmarch.com/#!newsletter/c1uhp) to sign up for my newsletter, and never miss another announcement about upcoming projects, new releases, sales, exclusive excerpts, and giveaways.

I'd love to hear what you thought about Holly and Creighton's story. If you have a few moments to leave a review, I'd be incredibly grateful. Send me a link at meghanmarchbooks@gmail.com, and I'll thank you with a personal note.

Also by Meghan March

THE DIRTY BILLIONAIRE Trilogy:
Dirty Billionaire
Dirty Pleasures
Dirty Together

BENEATH Series:
Beneath This Mask
Beneath This Ink
Beneath These Chains
Beneath These Scars

FLASH BANG Series:
Flash Bang
Hard Charger

Author's Note

I'd love to hear from you. Connect with me at:

UNAPOLOGETICALLY SEXY ROMANCE

Website: www.meghanmarch.com

Facebook: www.facebook.com/MeghanMarchAuthor

Twitter: www.twitter.com/meghan_march

Instagram: www.instagram.com/meghanmarch

ABOUT  THE AUTHOR

Meghan March has been known to wear camo face paint and tromp around in the woods wearing mud-covered boots, all while sporting a perfect manicure. She's also impulsive, easily entertained, and absolutely unapologetic about the fact that she loves to read and write smut.

Her past lives include slinging auto parts, selling lingerie, making custom jewelry, and practicing corporate law. Writing books about dirty-talking alpha males and the strong, sassy women who bring them to their knees is by far the most fabulous job she's ever had.

She loves hearing from her readers at:
meghanmarchbooks@gmail.com

38503451R00107

Made in the USA
Columbia, SC
05 December 2018